PANCAKES AND CORPSES

PERIDALE CAFE MYSTERY SERIES - BOOK 1

AGATHA FROST

pink tree

PUBLISHING

ALSO BY AGATHA FROST

Claire's Candles

1. Vanilla Bean Vengeance

2. Black Cherry Betrayal

Peridale Cafe

Book 1-10 Boxset

1. Pancakes and Corpses

2. Lemonade and Lies

3. Doughnuts and Deception

4. Chocolate Cake and Chaos

5. Shortbread and Sorrow

6. Espresso and Evil

7. Macarons and Mayhem

8. Fruit Cake and Fear

9. Birthday Cake and Bodies

10. Gingerbread and Ghosts

11.Cupcakes and Casualties

1

*B*aking was Julia South's therapy. As she squeezed more lemon juice into the buttercream icing, and avoided looking at the divorce papers sitting on her kitchen counter, she was grateful for that therapy more than ever.

"Good morning," she said to her smoky grey Maine Coon, Mowgli, as he strutted into the kitchen from the garden. "Hungry?"

Mowgli jumped onto the counter to greet her, making sure to cover the envelope containing the divorce papers with his muddy paw prints. Julia licked buttercream off her finger, and tickled appreciatively under his chin. He purred and rubbed his head against her, making her realise she wasn't just grateful for baking this morning.

Julia emptied a pouch of cat food into Mowgli's bowl as he softly purred and circled her feet. She tickled his head one last time before washing her hands and returning to her baking, just in time for the oven to beep.

Julia pulled out the lemon sponge cake and probed it with the end of a knife, delighted by how perfectly cooked it was. She removed it from the tray and set it on a cooling rack so it would be ready for the freshly made lemon buttercream icing. Julia had been working on the recipe for her new lemon sponge cake for the best part of the week, and she was sure she had found the right balance between tangy and sweet with her latest batch. Even if she approved of the cake, it wouldn't make its way onto her café's menu until her customers had taken their turns sampling it.

Leaving the cake to cool, Julia turned her attention to the thick envelope again. She reached out to pick it up, but stopped herself. Ever since it landed on her doormat three days ago, it had sat untouched in the same spot on her kitchen counter. She knew she needed to open it eventually, but she didn't want to ruin her Saturday morning, so she shook out her curls and wandered in to her bedroom.

Julia lived in a quaint, two-bedroom cottage in the tiny village of Peridale, in the heart of the Cotswolds. She had been born and raised in Peridale, and it had been her home until she met her soon-to-be ex-husband, Jerrad, at the age of twenty-one. She had moved to London to be with him, where she lived until two years ago, when Jerrad politely informed her that they would be divorcing so he could marry his blonde twenty-five-year-old secretary, Chantelle. She had entertained the idea of staying in the big city to make it on her own, but the lure of home had been too strong, so she sunk her life savings into the tiny cottage.

She quickly dressed and assessed herself in the mirror. She brushed flour out of her brown curls as well as the creases out of her mint coloured 1940s style dress. It covered the tops of her arms, nipped in at the waist, and flared out into a skirt that stopped just below her knees. She had twenty pounds on Chantelle, as well as ten years in age, but Julia didn't care; she had never been happier.

After icing the lemon sponge with the butter-cream, she boxed up the cake, and scratched Mowgli's cheek. He was sitting on the white envelope, hiding it from view with his fluffy behind. She liked to think he was hiding it on purpose, so she thanked him with a quick kiss on the head.

"See you later," she called to him, as she flung her handbag over her shoulder and grabbed her car keys. "Be good!"

The cool February sun shone down pleasantly on Julia as she hurried across her immaculate garden. A couple of the daffodils had sprouted early, adding some much needed bursts of yellow after a long and bitter winter.

She ducked into her vintage aqua blue Ford Anglia, dumping her handbag on the back seat, and her cake on the front. As though it was a small child, she pulled the seatbelt across the box before slotting her keys into the ignition. The car eased into first and she set off down the winding lane towards the heart of the village.

Julia's cottage was one of the last cottages on the edge of the village before the winding lane gave way to Peridale Farm, which sprawled onto miles and miles of uninterrupted countryside. She passed the next cottage dotted on the lane, and waved to Emily Burns, who waved back as she indulged in a spot of early morning gardening. The next cottage on the road had been empty for almost a year since Todrick Hamilton died. Julia usually cast her attention to the other side of the road so as not to stir up the still raw emotions of losing her elderly neighbour, but today she looked at Todrick's cottage because there was a large white van parked up outside it blocking the road. She slowed down until she could go no further, and pulled on the stiff handbrake. The door to the cottage was wide open, with furniture and boxes littering the small, messy garden.

Leaving her keys in the ignition and cake on the passenger seat, Julia got out of her car and walked over to the low stone wall surrounding the garden. As she did, a tall man ducked through the front door, shielding his eyes from the sun. He was wearing faded denim jeans with a simple white t-shirt. His hair was dark, with flecks of grey prickling the edges of his hairline. Julia would have put him in his late-thirties if she were a betting woman. The stranger dropped his hand and looked in her direction, and Julia was taken aback by how handsome he was. He hooked his thumbs into his jeans and walked towards her, an easy smile on his face and a slight pinch between his brows.

"Can I help you?" he asked, his voice deep and husky.

"I need to get through," Julia said, casting a finger to the van, suddenly feeling flustered.

"No problem" he said, his smile widening. "You local?"

"I live just up the road."

"I guess we're neighbours." The stranger walked over to the open gate and instead of going straight to the van, he walked over to Julia with an outstretched hand. "Barker. Barker Brown."

"Julia South," she said, accepting his firm handshake. "Welcome to Peridale. The clouds have cleared for your first day of village life."

People in Peridale talked about the weather a lot, which was a sign of not much else happening. Julia tried to avoid the subject at all costs because it was all she heard all day in her café, but she was a Peridale girl, born and bred, so the weather seemed to be her default conversation setting.

Barker nodded his thanks of her welcome and let go of her hand. Her comment about the weather didn't start the conversation she had hoped. Barker smiled at her, but it didn't seem like a friendly smile. He seemed slightly amused, and Julia couldn't help but feel judged by her new neighbour. Julia could practically smell the big city on him.

Barker pulled the van into a curve in the road, and Julia just stared for a moment, wondering what could have brought the man to the village. She hadn't spotted a wedding ring, but she knew it could easily be in his pocket. Trying not to overthink it, she jumped back into her own car. Barker climbed out of the van, walked back, and leaned his hand against the top of her car. Julia reluctantly rolled her window down.

"I'll see you around, Julie," Barker said, slapping the roof of her car.

"It's *Julia*."

"Right," he said with a nod, as though it didn't matter to him either way. "Bye."

Barker turned around and headed back into his cottage without a second look back at her. If it hadn't been for the car slowly pulling up behind her, she didn't know how long she would have stared at the cottage before driving away.

Julia tried not to be a judgemental person, but nothing about Barker seemed to fit Peridale. She couldn't put her finger on exactly why, but the man left a sour taste in her mouth.

Julia PULLED UP INTO THE TIGHT ALLEY BETWEEN HER café and the post office. Grabbing her cake and handbag, she squeezed out of the car and walked around to the front door. Her café was situated in the perfect place, right in the middle of the village, which directly faced the village green. The village's main shopping street, Mulberry Lane, was only a minute's walk away, meaning she was close enough to the action to entice the villagers without having to be in the middle of the action. A terraced row of cottages sat on the opposite side of the green, one of which was owned by her gran, Dot. St. Peter's Church and the small cemetery filled one of the other sides, with a row of two shops opposite, both of which were closed and boarded up. On the way to Mulberry Lane, there was the pub, The Plough, the B&B, ran by the eccentric mystic, Evelyn Wood, and the small local police station.

Julia walked into her dark café, instantly noticing something was wrong. She put her handbag and cake down on the nearest table and hurried across to the counter. Not for the first time that month, her cake stand had been ransacked, with only the crumbs left behind as evidence of yesterday's baking. She checked the backdoor, but it was still locked and there were no signs of forced entry.

"THE CAKES WERE GONE AGAIN THIS MORNING," JULIA said to her sister, Sue, who turned up for her usual Saturday shift to help out in the café. "Every last one."

"How many times is that now?" Sue asked as she secured her pale pink apron in place.

"Four," Julia said as she pulled a fresh batch of chocolate chip cookies out of the oven.

"I keep telling you to go to the police."

"For stolen cakes?" Julia slid the warm cookies onto a cooling rack and started shaping the next batch. "Do you think people will mind that I'm only selling cookies today? It's the quickest thing I could think of to fill up the display case."

"People will love whatever you put out there. Everybody knows you're the best baker in Peridale." Sue cut herself a slice of Julia's new lemon sponge cake. "Maybe it was rats?"

"How would a rat get up to the top shelf in that display case?"

"Super rats?" Sue said seriously with a shrug before taking a bite of the lemon sponge. "Ugh, this is so good. You're ruining my diet."

Sue had been on a constant diet for as long as Julia could remember, despite her younger sister having a svelte figure that most women would kill for.

"Who breaks into a café and only takes the cakes?" Julia mumbled under her breath as she moulded a ball of dough into a flat disc.

"Stop leaving the cakes in here overnight," Sue said through a mouthful of lemon sponge. "They'll soon get the message."

"I have a feeling it's somebody who needs the food."

"Call the police."

"I don't have any evidence."

"I think it's time for some cameras," Sue said as she licked buttercream icing from her fingers, before casting a finger into the corners of the rooms. "It's also time to hire some real staff. You know I've enjoyed helping you out on the weekends, but I can't keep turning down the extra shifts at the hospital for much longer."

Julia's stomach squirmed. The '*HELP WANTED*' sign had been in the window since the beginning of the year but it hadn't generated much interest. Most people in Peridale either owned their own small business in the village, or they commuted to the bigger towns for work. The rest were retired, which suited Julia and her café. She was never short of customers wanting a slice of cake, a cup of tea, and a friendly chat.

When the cookies were finished, Julia flipped the sign from '*Sorry! We're closed*' to '*Come on in! We're open!*', and it wasn't long until her first customer and closest neighbour, Emily Burns, walked in, still wearing her gardening gloves.

"Cup of tea when you're ready, Julia," she said as she sat down at the table nearest the counter. "And a slice of whatever that cake is on the counter. Smells delicious."

Julia made up a small pot of tea and cut a slice of the lemon sponge, while Sue finished making the cookies for the day in the kitchen.

"The cake is on the house," Julia said, setting the plate in front of Emily. "It's a new recipe I'm working on, and honest feedback is welcomed."

"You haven't disappointed me yet!" Emily exclaimed. "Have you seen our new neighbour?"

Emily asked the question so casually, but Julia

knew Emily had probably been peeking over her garden wall to witness Julia's interaction with Barker. If talking about the weather was the number one topic of choice in Peridale, gossiping about fellow villagers was the second. Julia wasn't much of a gossip, but it was rare she wasn't one of the first to find out the latest information, thanks to her café.

"I had a brief conversation with him this morning," Julia said, taking up a seat across from Emily and pouring a cup of tea from the pot. "He's called Barker Brown. I think he's from the city."

"Oh really?" Emily mumbled, her eyes widening at the new information. "He's rather handsome. If only I was twenty years younger."

"I hadn't noticed," Julia lied, adding a splash of milk and a spoonful of sugar to her tea. "Do you know why he's here?"

Much to Julia's disappointment, Emily shook her head as she took her first bite of the lemon sponge. Her eyes widened even further than before, and then clenched shut as she savoured the citrusy tang of the cake.

"Oh, Julia!" Emily exclaimed. "You've really outdone yourself with this one! I think this might be my new favourite."

"Thank you," Julia said quickly, wanting to get back to the topic of their new neighbour. "I'm not sure about Barker. He seemed a little smug."

Julia sipped her own tea as she tried to figure out why the man had had such an effect on her.

"The handsome ones usually are." Emily sighed regretfully. "Maybe he's retired young."

"Maybe," Julia agreed, not really believing it. "He doesn't strike me as the type of person who would choose a place like Peridale to retire."

They both finished their tea and Emily settled her bill to get back to her gardening. Julia knew she would try to strike up a conversation with Barker, if only to extract some information worth gossiping about on their next meeting. Even though Julia wouldn't usually be privy to joining in, she was more than intrigued by his sudden arrival.

The moment she resumed her place behind the counter, the bell above the door rang again. This time, it was Roxy Carter, an old friend from school. They had been amongst the few girls from the village in their class at the local comprehensive, Hollins High School, so they struck up a close friendship that had lasted long into adulthood. Roxy now worked as a teacher in Peridale's only school, St. Peter's Primary School.

"Good morning, Roxy," Julia said with a smile as Roxy approached the counter. "What can I get you today?"

"Huh?" Roxy mumbled, staring at Julia as though she had no idea where she was.

Roxy frantically ran her fingers through her red hair, tucking it messily behind her ears. Her eyes were sunken in and her skin pasty, as though she hadn't slept well for days.

"Is everything okay?" Julia asked.

Roxy blinked hard at Julia and glanced up at the chalkboard menu on the wall behind her.

"Latte to go please," Roxy said, shaking her head heavily. "I'm fine, just a little tired. You know what it's like."

Julia dug out a cardboard cup from underneath the counter and walked over to the coffee machine, not taking her eyes away from Roxy. Julia was used to her friend's heavy sarcasm and cheeky wit, but none of that was present today. Roxy chomped on the edges of her nails and jumped when the coffee machine hissed into life. Julia didn't need to ask again to know Roxy wasn't '*fine*.'

"Why don't you take a seat and I'll bring it over to you?" Julia offered.

Roxy nodded and picked the table closest to the counter, just like Emily had. Julia poured the steamed milk into the coffee and pressed the plastic lid securely in place. She placed the cup in front of Roxy, who stopped drumming her fingers to pick up the cup. She took a deep sip, not seeming to notice it was hot.

"Are you sure you're okay?" Julia asked softly, reaching across and resting her hand on top of Roxy's. "You seem a little on edge."

Roxy tried to feign a smile, but her bottom lip wobbled to the point where Julia reached into her dress pocket for her handkerchief. She pushed it across the table to Roxy, who gladly accepted it and dabbed the inner corners of her eyes.

"I'm just being silly," Roxy said, trying to force a laugh. "Ignore me."

"Silly is okay," Julia said reassuringly. "A problem shared is a problem halved."

Roxy smiled genuinely this time and pushed the handkerchief back to Julia, but Julia didn't pocket it straight away, just in case it was needed again. A car sped past the café and Roxy almost jumped out of her skin.

"Oh, Julia," Roxy whispered, leaning in low across the table. "I've ruined everything."

Before Julia could ask what she had ruined, a loud clatter, followed by Sue's loud cursing, came from the kitchen.

"Stay here," Julia said. "I'll be back in two seconds."

Roxy nodded and looked down at her coffee, her eyes glazing over. Julia hated to leave her, but Sue sounded like she was in trouble, and Julia's mind went straight to her mystery cake burglar.

"What's wrong?" Julia asked, dashing through the beaded curtains to the brightly lit kitchen. "I bet they heard that halfway across the village."

Sue used the counter to help herself up from the floor, where two metal trays of cookies and fresh dough surrounded her.

"I saw a spider," Sue moaned, pushing her thick brown curls from her eyes. "It ran right across the counter!"

"Is that all?"

"I could have died!"

Julia chuckled and sighed. She leaned over and

picked up the mess as her sister straightened herself out.

"If only Mowgli was here," Julia said as she scraped the dough into the bin. "He loves chasing spiders."

"You know I'm allergic to cats."

"You're not allergic, you just don't like them," Julia teased. "If you see it again, call me to catch it, instead of throwing my cookies on the floor."

Julia patted her little sister on the shoulder and walked back into the café. Roxy was still there, but she wasn't in her seat. She was standing by the door with Gertrude Smith, the elderly organist from St. Peter's Church. Roxy was clutching Gertrude's arms and her face was screwed up as though she was about to say something unsavoury. They both looked over to Julia, and Roxy immediately let go of Gertrude and stormed out of the café, leaving behind her latte.

"Quite rude!" Gertrude exclaimed as she straightened out the sleeves of her coat. "What a *horrible* girl!"

"Is everything okay?" Julia frowned, looking from Gertrude to the latte.

"That girl is *unhinged!*" Gertrude cried, loud enough so that the whole village could hear. "*Unstable!*"

Gertrude came into the café every morning at ten for her usual pancakes and tea, even if Julia had to pretend she didn't notice the regularity of the organist's visits. The one time Julia had attempted to surprise Gertrude by having her order ready for her at ten, Gertrude had made sure to give Julia quite the dressing down, telling Julia she shouldn't be so presumptive. That had been over a year ago, and even though Gertrude claimed she might have wanted to order something else on the day Julia had pre-empted her order, she still hadn't ordered anything other than her usual since.

"Four pancakes, American-style, drizzled with honey, with fresh raspberries and blueberries, and a cup of tea," Gertrude called across the café as she took her usual seat at the table next to the window. "And when I say fresh, I mean *fresh*!"

Julia smiled and nodded, biting her tongue. She had just enough blueberries and raspberries delivered to her café every morning, just for Gertrude's order. Sue didn't understand why Julia bent over backwards to please such an intolerable woman, but Julia knew her livelihood balanced on the knife-edge of her reputation, and a negative comment from

Gertrude would spread like wildfire around the tiny village in a matter of hours.

After making the pancakes and tea, Julia carefully set them in front of Gertrude. She usually turned her nose up at the food, as though she didn't return everyday, but today, she stared out of the window, completely distracted. Julia cleared her throat and Gertrude jumped, looking down at her food. Julia usually hurried away, but she hovered.

"Yes?" Gertrude said through pursed lips. "Can I help you?"

Julia's cheeks burned and her mouth turned dry. She looked out of the window at the village green, which had filled up with young children enjoying the first day of the weekend.

"Is there something happening between you and Roxy Carter?" Julia asked, as bravely as she could.

"I don't see what business that is of yours, *girl*!"

And with that, Julia scurried back to the kitchen, to vent to Sue.

"Somebody is going to kill that woman one day," Sue whispered, peeking through the beads as Gertrude tucked into her pancakes. "Mark my words."

2

The rest of Julia's day went by a lot smoother than her morning had. Her lemon sponge cake was a hit with everybody who tasted it and she sold out of all of her cookies.

During the week, Julia had to invent little jobs to kill the time between customers, which was why she loved Saturdays so much. Along with her usual daily customers, she also got to see her weekend customers and converse with the tourists and groups of ramblers enjoying the Cotswolds.

An hour before closing, her gran, Dot, hurried into the full café, wearing her usual stiff white shirt, buttoned up to her chin that was secured in place with an ornate antique brooch. She looked around at the faces, smiling at the villagers she knew and narrowing her eyes suspiciously at the ones she didn't.

"Have you heard about the new man?" Dot asked the second she reached the counter. "It's causing quite the scandal!"

"Hello, Gran," Julia said. "Cup of tea?"

"No thanks," Dot said, glancing over her shoulder at the full café. "You know how I hate big crowds, love. Did you hear about the new man?"

"Do you mean Barker Brown who moved into the cottage on my lane?"

"So, you *have* heard?" Dot sighed, clearly disappointed that she hadn't been the first to break the news. "Why didn't you tell me?"

"That I'd met my new neighbour?"

"You've spoken to him?" Dot's eyes widened. "What did he have to say for himself?"

"Not a lot. His van was blocking the road so I asked him to move it. We introduced ourselves and spoke briefly."

"Spoke about what?" Dot urged.

"The weather," Julia lied, not wanting to admit he had ignored her weather based conversation starter. "What was I supposed to talk to him about?"

"About why he bought Todrick Hamilton's cottage at auction for half of the asking price!" Dot cried, loud enough to catch the attention of the people in the café. "Todrick's daughter, Samantha, is said to be furious. She wasn't getting any offers, so she put it up for auction, expecting to get a decent amount. *No!* That slime from the city came in and scooped it up for nothing."

"So, he is from the city?"

"That's what Emily Burns says."

"Emily got that information from me," Julia said with a soft laugh. "I was only speculating."

"Well, it's all the village has been talking about all morning. I heard he was a business tycoon who had come in to buy up all of the companies and turn us into some kind of tourist hot spot! Can you imagine?"

The tourists in the shop frowned at Dot, who was now directing all of her statements loudly into her listening crowd.

"Where did you hear that?" Julia asked.

"Well, it's what I suspect!" Dot cried, snapping her fingers together. "I better go. I've got topside of beef in the oven. You and your sister are having supper at mine tonight."

Julia didn't argue. Even if she had plans, she

would have to cancel them. It didn't matter how old she or Sue got, they couldn't ignore a supper summons from their gran.

Without another word, Dot turned on her heels and teetered back out of the café, her navy blue pleated skirt floating behind her. Julia hoped she would have just half of her gran's zest for life when she reached her eighties.

"We're having supper at Gran's tonight," Julia said, poking her head through the beads. "Oh, hello, Johnny. What are you doing here?"

Julia left the full café and walked through to the kitchen, where Johnny Watson was talking in low whispers with Sue. Johnny was a reporter for the local newspaper, *The Peridale Post*. Julia had been on an unsuccessful date with him when she first moved back to the village. They had gone for coffee outside the village where she had decided they would be better suited as friends. Sue was insistent that Johnny still held a candle for Julia, but she brushed off her sister's unfounded gossip.

"Julia," Johnny said nervously, his cheeks reddening. "It's you I came to see."

Sue looked awkwardly at her, as though she knew something Julia didn't. When Sue looked down at the piece of paper in Johnny's hands, Julia followed her, and her heart sank.

"Is everything okay?" Julia asked, trying to keep her smile.

"I tried to stop them from printing it," Johnny said. "I really did try, but they wouldn't listen to me."

"Print what?"

"Maybe it's better she doesn't read it," Sue said.

"Read what?"

Johnny looked down at the paper in his hands. He seemed to be toying with his conscience for a moment before handing the paper over to Julia. She looked at Johnny, who looked apologetically at her as he shifted his glasses, before looking down at what was causing her sister to look so uncomfortable.

"'*Local Café Is A Constant Disappointment*'," Julia said, reading the headline of what appeared to be a review. "'*Two stars*'. This is about my café?"

"Oh, Julia," Sue said, placing her hand on Julia's shoulder. "It's just somebody's opinion."

"Who wrote this?" Julia asked as she scanned through the review. "'*Awful atmosphere*,' '*bland food*', '*amateur baking*'!"

Julia's heart sank to the pit of her stomach, and she cast the paper onto the counter.

"I have no idea," Johnny said, looking as upset as Julia felt. "Our old reviewer, Mark Tanner, retired last month and we put out an ad for somebody to take his place. We only had one reply, and it came with the condition they would have full anonymity, even from us. We didn't have much choice. This is only their third review, but they haven't given one above a two-star. They gave Rachel Carter's art gallery a one-star review, saying '*the only art the gallery could offer you was something to toss on the fire on a cold night*', and they gave Bob and Shelby Hopkins a two-star for The Plough, saying it was '*the worst pub in the Cotswolds*' and that their home brewed beer tasted like something '*left over in the sink after washing up*'. I've been fighting this all week, but my editor thinks it adds spice to the paper. When I found out it was going to print tomorrow, I came straight here to warn you."

Julia stared down at the paper, numb and shaken. She had always been confident with her café and what she served in it. When working in London, she had worked in a factory, bulk baking bland cakes for retail for most of her marriage, which was why she had tried so hard to create something that was the opposite of that.

"It's tomorrow's fish and chip's paper," Sue said encouragingly. "Don't let it get to you."

Julia tried to smile, but the corners of her mouth wouldn't turn upwards. She racked her brain for whom she could have upset for them to write such a bitter review.

"Thank you for warning me," Julia said to Johnny. "Can I keep this?"

"Only if you're sure. Like Sue said, it's tomorrow's chip paper."

Julia wanted to agree but she knew how long a single topic could circulate the village when there was nothing more interesting to talk about. If the weather held up and didn't rain, it would be the only thing to gossip about, aside from the new arrival. She doubted anything could eclipse such a juicy review of the village's only café.

"Do you know anything about who it could be?" Julia asked as she scanned the review, not really taking the words in.

"They only correspond by letter, but it's always hand delivered in the dead of night," Johnny said as he put his hands into his coat pocket. "It's always signed '*Miss Piston*', but we think it's an alias, because there's nobody in this village with that name."

Julia thanked Johnny again, and he left through the backdoor. Sue attempted to take the review away from Julia but she read it over and over, absorbing every word. She was only pulled from the writing when the bell on the counter rang.

For the rest of her work day, Julia attempted to smile through her pain, but it wasn't enough. Every customer who knew Julia could tell something was wrong, but just like Roxy had with her, she lied and said she was fine. None of them believed her, which was why she was glad when half-past five rolled around and she could lock the door and flip the sign.

As Julia cleared away the plates, she could feel the sympathetic eyes of her sister watching her.

"People in this village will know it is all lies," said Sue. "You're the best baker in Peridale! Whoever wrote this was just jealous."

"Maybe."

"Don't let it get to you."

"I'm not."

"Liar," Sue said as Julia walked past her with a stack of plates and cups. "Whoever Miss Piston is, they're probably really unhappy and that's why they have to bring other people down."

Julia dumped the dishes in the sink and filled it

with hot, soapy water. As she cleaned the plates and cups, Sue wiped down the tables, leaving her to her own thoughts. She imagined opening up on Monday morning after being closed tomorrow. She knew people wouldn't avoid the café, in fact, she would probably be busier than ever, but she knew every customer would be clutching a copy of the newspaper, all with their own thoughts and opinions about the review. They would all be waiting for her reaction from the moment they read it.

"At least we've got Gran's topside of beef to take your mind off of it," Sue said as they pulled on their coats. "I just need to call Neil and let him know not to expect me home until late."

Sue hurried over to the phone behind the counter, leaving Julia to flick off the lights. She buttoned up her pale pink pea coat in the dark as her sister called her husband. If she didn't feel obligated, she would have cancelled supper at Gran's to go home to Mowgli and curl up in front of the TV with dinner for one, even if she did have her divorce papers taunting her.

As she waited for Sue, she reflected on what a strange day it had been. She thought back to Roxy, and her peculiar interaction with Gertrude. She made a mental note to call Roxy when she got to her gran's, just to make sure she was okay.

"I asked Neil if he knew any Pistons," Sue said as she weaved back through the tables. "No luck, but he said he'll check the records at the library tomorrow."

Julia's brows pinched together, but not at her sister, at something she had said.

"Pistons," Julia murmured.

"Huh?"

"Organ pistons!" Julia cried, pushing her keys into Sue's hands. "Lock up and tell Gran I'll be there in twenty minutes. I think I know who wrote that review."

Before Sue could ask any questions, Julia hurried across the village to confront the local organist.

GERTRUDE SMITH'S COTTAGE HAD ALWAYS BEEN A TOPIC of discussion. Julia remembered the terror it inflicted on her when she had to walk past it on her way home from St. Peter's Primary School as a small girl. It was a small cottage, not dissimilar from her own, but it had been swallowed up by so much creeping ivy, only the door and two windows were visible under the low hanging thatched roof. The small walled-in front garden was equally overgrown, and despite many villagers confronting Gertrude about it over the years, she refused to change a thing, insisting it was '*God's will*' to let the plants grow as naturally as possible.

As a thirty-seven-year-old woman, Julia agreed that the cottage was an eyesore in the otherwise spotless and orderly village, but it still inflicted the same childhood fear in the pit of her stomach.

Gertrude's cottage was in the middle of a row of six other small cottages. It didn't just stand out for the lack of a well-kept garden, it was also the only cottage on the street without a single light on in the house.

Julia stayed in the safety of the streetlight, staring at Gertrude's cottage. It didn't look like she was home, so Julia decided she was going to leave her conversation with Gertrude until Monday morning, when Gertrude would no doubt be in for her raspberry and blueberry pancakes to see the aftermath of her review. In the glow of the streetlight, she pulled out the review and read over it again, noticing how she was getting increasingly more wound up with each re-read. She looked up angrily at the cottage and noticed a shadow dart past the window.

Inhaling deeply, Julia unhooked the gate and

waited for Gertrude to flick on a lamp, but the cottage remained in darkness. Julia glanced up and down the dark street, but it was completely empty. She could hear the six o'clock news playing on the television of one of the neighbours, but aside from that, there was an eerie silence she hadn't experienced before in the village she loved so much.

Julia walked down the short garden path, stepping over the plants that had snaked across the stone slabs. She reached the front door and rapped her knuckles against the old wood; the door opened upon impact.

Startled by the movement, Julia took a step back and peered into the cottage, wondering why Gertrude would leave her front door open.

"*Gertrude*?" Julia called into the dark. "It's Julia, from the café."

Julia heard sudden movement and the smash of glass, followed by more of the eerie silence that made her feel so uncomfortable.

"Gertrude?" she called out again, pushing on the door and opening it fully. "Do you need some help?"

There wasn't a response, so Julia hesitantly stepped over the threshold and into Gertrude's living room. The inside matched the outside, with dark floral prints lining the walls, equally dark colours for the flooring, and an array of photographs and ornaments among the bulky cluttered furniture.

Julia almost called out again, but she stopped herself. She walked through the open double doors to the dining room. The broken window caught Julia's attention, as did the almost complete lack of glass on the table underneath it.

Holding her breath, she turned, wanting to run straight for the street, but an open door leading off from the dining room caught her attention. Through the shadows, she noticed a figure in a chair. A relieved sigh left her lips and she relaxed for a moment. Squinting into the dark, it looked like whoever was in there was hunched over the desk writing something in the dark.

Julia pushed on the door, and it opened slowly. A strip of moonlight shone from the smashed window, illuminating the room. Even without the light, she had recognised Gertrude's tightly roller set hair, but she hadn't spotted something large and sharp jutting out from between Gertrude's shoulder blades.

Julia inhaled deeper than she thought she could as the moonlight glittered against the tiny part of the knife that hadn't been sunk into Gertrude's flesh. Her eyes flitted to Gertrude's glossy wide eyes and her slightly ajar mouth. Gertrude was still clutching a pen in her pale fingers. Julia attempted to scream, but no sound left her trembling lips.

Knowing there was nothing she could do for Gertrude, Julia ran back through the cottage and into the safety of the streetlight.

"I need the police," Julia said frantically into her phone as she choked back the tears. "There's been a murder."

3

*D*ot's cottage was one of the few constants threading through Julia's life. It had been there for the little girl who had struggled with the death of her mother, and it had been there for that same girl when she was in her thirties and her marriage had broken down. Julia appreciated her gran's opposition to change. Dot still had the same eleven-inch black and white television she had always had, the same floral sofa she refused to replace, and the same collection of ceramic cats, which Dot dusted every day, looking out from her mantelpiece.

Julia moved the beef around the gravy on her plate, and wondered why for the first time in her life the cottage wasn't providing that same safety and comfort.

"You need to eat something, love," Dot said calmly, resting her hand on Julia's. "You need to keep your strength up."

"I can't stop thinking about that knife," Julia said. "It was so big."

"That poor woman," Sue said, who also appeared to be struggling to eat. "You'd be pushed to find anybody who liked her, but that's no way to die."

"You reap what you sow in this life," Dot said, tapping her finger on the wood. "Let this be a lesson to all of us. Gertrude was a nasty piece of work, I'm just surprised it's taken this long for somebody to do her in."

Julia and Sue both looked wide-eyed at each other, before turning to their gran, who pursed her lips without apology.

"Let's not pretend she wasn't the woman who wrote those nasty things about your café, Julia!" Dot stabbed her finger down on the piece of paper on the table. "Utter rubbish!"

There was a knock at the door. Glad of the distraction, Julia jumped up and hurried down the dark hallway. She passed a mirror and her pale complexion caught her attention. She was sure the colour would never return to her cheeks.

Inhaling deeply, she opened the door. A tall man loomed in the doorway, facing out towards the village green. Julia cleared her throat and the man spun around. It took Julia a second to recognise the man as her new neighbour, Barker Brown. He had swapped his faded jeans and white t-shirt for a well-fitting suit and a beige overcoat, which was turned up at the collar. His face was just as handsome.

Barker frowned down at her, with the same amused smile from earlier in the day.

"Julia *South*?" Barker asked, checking a notepad in his hands, as though he hadn't remembered her name from their first conversation.

"Yes?"

"Detective Inspector Brown." He reached out his hand, a dark twinkle in his eyes. "I hear you discovered the body of a Mrs Gertrude Smith. May I come in and ask you a few questions?"

JULIA SAT IN THE MIDDLE OF THE COMFORTABLE SOFA and Detective Inspector Brown filled up one of Dot's tiny armchairs. He looked around the small cottage with the same amused smile Julia had come to know him by. It made her stomach squirm uncomfortably.

"Tea!" Dot exclaimed, hurrying in with a tray, containing what Julia knew to be her finest china teapot and cups.

Dot set the tray on the table and retreated to the back of the room, where she stayed until Barker cleared his throat. She scurried back through to the dining room, where she and Sue would no doubt be pushing glasses up against the wall to overhear every word.

"You told the officers on the scene that you were walking home and saw a shadow in the window, and the open door?" Barker asked after consulting his small notepad. "Long way to walk home, isn't it? Forgive me because I don't know my way around the village yet, but isn't your cottage on the opposite side?"

Julia shifted in her seat and picked invisible lint off of her mint coloured dress, wondering why she had lied about her intentions behind visiting Gertrude. She pulled the hem past her knees and straightened out her back, deciding honesty was the best policy.

"I was going to see Gertrude to ask her a question," Julia said, avoiding admitting to her lie. "I saw the figure and I assumed it was Gertrude. I walked up to the door and I knocked, but the door swung open, and then I heard glass smashing. I thought she might be in trouble, so I called out for Gertrude, but she didn't respond, so I went inside to see if she was okay. I saw the broken window and I decided I was going to get out of there, to call the police, and that's when I saw her body."

Julia tried to stay strong but she felt the tears welling up in the corners of her eyes. She plucked her handkerchief from her pocket and quickly dabbed them away, not wanting to appear weak in front of the detective.

"I understand it's a difficult time for you," Barker said, completely devoid of any emotion. "What can you tell me about the shadow you claim to have seen?"

Julia was taken aback by the insinuation that her story wasn't true. It suddenly struck her that she was possibly a suspect.

"I don't know," Julia said, trying her best to focus on the blurry image in her mind. "It was dark. There were no lights on in the cottage. I just saw movement, called out, and then I heard the glass smash. Perhaps they were going to leave out of the front door, and then they saw or heard me so they panicked and escaped through the window?"

"Why don't we leave the speculating to the police?" Barker arched a brow and appeared to be concealing his amused smile. "You said you were going to ask Gertrude a question. What was that question?"

Julia told him all about how Johnny Watson had visited her café to tell her about Miss Piston's venomous review, and how she had made the connection between piston and organ.

"Organ?"

"Gertrude plays the organ at the local church," she said. "*Played* the organ. She's done it for as long as I can remember."

"So you put two and two together and discovered a body?" Barker mumbled, and Julia was unsure if the question was rhetorical or not. "Is there anything else you can tell me about Gertrude Smith? Do you know who could have done this?"

Julia's mind flashed straight to Roxy Carter, and their meeting in her café that morning. She couldn't believe she was considering one of her oldest friends could be capable of murder, but it was something she was considering. She decided she would tell Detective Inspector Brown this piece of information, but only after she had had a chance to speak with Roxy herself.

"Gertrude comes into my café every morning at ten," Julia said. "She has four pancakes with honey, raspberries and blueberries and a cup of tea."

"I was looking for something less *trivial*," Barker said with a sigh. "About her relationships or her affairs."

Julia pursed her lips and adjusted herself in the seat once more. She wanted to give the Detective a piece of her mind, but she was aware she was the only person who had any real information about the murder and she was her own alibi, so she bit her tongue.

"She has a son. William."

"Any friends?"

"Gertrude wasn't the type of woman to have friends," Julia said. "She was deeply religious and she didn't suffer fools gladly."

"So you're saying she had enemies?"

"I wouldn't go that far," Julia said, disliking how Barker could so easily twist her words. "I just know that she's upset a lot of people in this village over the years."

"And you're one of them," he added.

"I suppose I am," she said, narrowing her eyes. "But not enough to murder her."

Detective Inspector Brown stood up, his head almost hitting the beams in the low ceiling. He pulled a card out of his inside pocket and handed it over to Julia. It contained his name, title, phone number, and the address of the village police station. She suspected they were freshly printed.

"You'll have to stop by the station tomorrow to make an official statement, but I'm satisfied with what you've told me," Baker said, sounding anything but satisfied. "If you think of anything at all, give me a call. I'll see myself out."

Barker opened the living room door, and Dot fell into him. She jumped back, straightened out the pleats in her skirt, and smiled politely.

"Thanks for the tea," he said, before turning back to face Julia. "Oh, and Julie, try not to find any more dead bodies, will you?"

"It's Julia."

"*Right*," Barker said, a small smile tickling his lips as he turned. "Goodnight."

Detective Inspector Brown left the cottage, but his presence lingered, as did his smile. Julia looked down at the business card and ran her fingers over his name. She resisted the urge to shred it into a million pieces. Barker had seemed more interested in point scoring than actually getting information from her. Tucking the business card into her dress pocket, she tried to figure out why that was.

"You're blushing," Sue said, jabbing Julia in the ribs. "I think you like him."

"*Like* him?" Julia scoffed. "The man is practically *intolerable*."

"But *quite* handsome," added Dot, seemingly forgetting her own gossip from earlier in the day. "Quite handsome *indeed*."

Julia couldn't bring herself to disagree with her gran.

LATER THAT NIGHT, JULIA CURLED UP BY THE FIRE IN her cottage with Mowgli at her feet. She sipped a cup of her favourite peppermint and liquorice tea and grabbed her ingredients list notepad from the side table.

She flipped past a list of things she needed to pick up to make a chocolate orange fudge cake and turned to a fresh page. She bit the lid off the pen and wrote '*Gertrude Smith*' in the centre of the small page. She circled the name until the ink tore a hole in the paper and ripped through to the next page.

After taking another sip of her tea, and letting the sweet liquorice coat her throat, she reluctantly drew an arrow from the circle and wrote '*Roxy Carter*'. She didn't want to think her oldest friend could be capable of murder, but she knew she had to prove otherwise.

"You're barking up the wrong tree, Barker," she whispered to herself as she carefully closed the notepad.

4

*P*eridale was a small village, so church attendance was slightly higher than most of the United Kingdom, but that didn't explain the circus Julia was witnessing at St. Peter's Church for its Sunday service.

"Everybody in the village has turned up," Dot whispered into Julia's ear as they shuffled into the crowded church. "There are only four reasons people have turned up today and three of them are connected to Gertrude's death!"

"Isn't that why we're here?" Julia whispered back. "I wouldn't have been here if you hadn't let yourself into my cottage this morning and shook me awake. I thought you were the murderer coming to get rid of the only witness!"

"I'm here every weekend!" Dot said, pursing her lips as she adjusted her finest church hat. "I come to pray. I'm a very religious woman, you know."

"Don't lie, Gran," Sue said, who was linking arms with Dot on the other side as they tried to find somewhere to stand. "You're usually fast asleep in bed when Sunday service is happening."

"*Shhh!* Not in God's house," Dot said, pointing up to the church's high ceiling. "What *He* doesn't know won't hurt *Him*. I'm here in spirit and I pray in my dreams."

"What do you pray for?" Sue asked.

"That He saves your souls, and that He brings a new man into Julia's life." Dot said, so loud that the people in the back row of the pews turned.

"I do *not* need a new man," Julia whispered, thinking instantly of the unopened divorce papers that were still waiting on her kitchen counter, waiting for her signature. "What are the four reasons that you think people are here?"

"Well," Dot said coyly, obviously glad Julia had asked, "I've given this a lot of thought. The first reason is that people are here to ask for protection from the murderer on the loose. The second is that the murderer is here asking for forgiveness and everybody is waiting for somebody to slip up."

That thought had crossed Julia's mind and it was one of the reasons she had rolled out of bed and crawled into her clothes. She had held Mowgli as close as he would allow last night, and the sun had already started to rise by the time she finally fell asleep. The image of the knife sticking out of Gertrude's back hadn't allowed her brain to stop trying to piece the puzzle together, no matter how tired she was.

"The third reason," Dot continued. "People are here to see who is taking over Gertrude's organ playing duties."

"I hadn't thought of that one," Sue gasped. "I wonder who it is."

"My money is on Amy Clark," Dot said, tapping her finger on her chin thoughtfully. "Everybody knows she's been after Gertrude's position for years. Gertrude is the far superior organist, which is why she hasn't missed a Sunday service in over forty years. She once dragged herself out of bed with the most terrible flu and still played amazingly. I wouldn't be surprised if Amy Clark was thanking God on her knees when she found out the news about poor Gertrude, God rest her soul."

"You've changed your tune from last night," Sue said, rolling her eyes.

"Not in the Lord's house," Dot said, nodding to the large statue of Jesus hanging from the cross at the front of the packed church. "The fourth reason is that people are genuinely here for the Sunday service."

Julia had to admit she wasn't one of them. She wasn't particularly religious, although she did believe something was out there, she just hadn't figured out what yet. The only times she attended church services were for christenings, weddings, funerals and Christmas Eve mass. She looked around the church, smiling to people she recognised, knowing most of them had only shown up for the first three of her gran's four reasons.

A fifth reason had also compelled Julia to attend the service, but she decided to keep it to herself. She wanted to see if Roxy Carter would turn up. When she had finally fallen asleep in the early hours of the morning, she had been plagued by a terrible nightmare of Roxy standing over her with a large knife, ready to strike her down.

Julia had already scanned the faces of the attendees sitting in the pews and Roxy Carter's bright red hair hadn't jumped out at her. She was naturally ginger, so when she applied the red dye over the top, it made it look like her hair was made from pure flames. Julia had always admired Roxy's bravery to go for such a bright colour, and even though Roxy pulled it off with ease, Julia couldn't see herself doing the same.

Turning her attention to the people still filing into the packed church, her heart skipped a beat when she noticed Roxy's sister, Rachel, followed by their mother, Imogen Carter. Julia waited for Roxy to follow Imogen, but she didn't. Her heart skipped another more intense beat when Detective Inspector Brown waltzed in behind them.

Julia quickly turned her attention to the front of the church, just in time to witness Amy Clark shuffling out of Father David Green's vestry. Julia didn't want to be cynical, but even from her distance she could see what could only be described as the second smuggest smile she had seen all weekend. She glanced to Barker Brown, the owner of the first, who was standing four people away from her, looming inches above everyone around him. Even though he too was staring ahead, she could feel him looking at her out of the corner of his eye.

Amy Clark walked over to the organ and unbuttoned her coat. She was wearing a bright pink woollen cardigan, a diamond brooch twinkling from its breast pocket, with a pale blue pleated skirt, tan tights and a pair of sensible black shoes. Her usually wild and frizzy hair had been pristinely set into neat curled rows, making Julia wonder if the hairdresser had opened specially for Amy that morning for her big appearance.

The second Amy sat down on the stool and cracked her fingers, the frantic whispering started. Julia watched as heads turned and eyes widened when her fingers touched the organ's keys. The whispering turned to talking and then to almost shouting as '*All Things Bright and Beautiful*' bellowed through the pipes. The noise from the congregation didn't fall until Father David walked out of his vestry with a sad smile on his face.

"Not as good as Gertrude," Dot said rather loudly

above the music. "Wolf in sheep's clothing. Amateur stuff!"

Father David delivered a lengthy and heartfelt eulogy for Gertrude, which caused more than a couple of people to clutch their tissues and hankies to their eyes. At one point, Father David even looked like he was going to shed a tear, but he held himself together. He ended his speech by commenting on the impressive turnout, and how he hadn't seen such a full church in his twenty years of service. The hint of sarcasm in his voice caused more than a couple of people to squirm in their seats, and if Julia had been sitting, she would have been one of them.

The service was longer than Julia had expected and it wasn't until almost an hour later that they were walking out of the church. The weather had perked up from the morning's clouds, but even though the sky was as clear as could be, it still felt like there was a dark cloud hanging over the village.

Dot and Sue walked arm in arm towards the church gates, but Julia told them to go ahead without her. Both of them looked back at her suspiciously, but they didn't object. She waited until Rachel and Imogen Carter exited and she caught their eyes through the crowd.

When they cut through and walked in her direction, she realised they also wanted to speak to her too.

"Julia, sweetheart," Imogen said softly, resting her hand on Julia's. "I hear you found the body. Terrible business all of this, isn't it?"

"It really is," Julia said, sighing heavily. "I was wondering if you've seen Roxy recently?"

"Why?" Imogen asked, clearly confused. "Should I have?"

Julia tried to keep her smile firmly on her face as she stared at Imogen, wondering if she should tell her everything she had witnessed the morning before. She decided against it.

"I just wanted to catch up with her, that's all," Julia lied, widening her smile so much she was sure it looked fake.

Imogen nodded, patted Julia's hands and said her goodbyes. Rachel hung back and told her mother they would meet in The Plough for lunch later that afternoon. Imogen waved to them both and scurried off, leaving Rachel and Julia alone outside the church.

Rachel Carter was the complete opposite of her sister Roxy, but still as sweet. Instead of having red hair, her hair was onyx black and her features slender. Rachel was one of the few people in the village who had left to pursue a university education, although she returned around the same time Julia did to put her fine art degree to good use by taking over the management of the local art gallery.

"Roxy told me about the argument with Gertrude Smith in the café yesterday morning," Rachel said in a hushed voice, glancing over her shoulder to make sure the passing crowd wasn't listening. "She was in a state."

"Have you seen her?"

Rachel shook her head, and grabbed Julia's arm and pulled her into the shadow of the large oak tree on the church grounds. When she seemed satisfied they were out of earshot of the lingering attendees, she looked deep into Julia's eyes.

"I haven't seen her since yesterday morning," Rachel said, biting into her orangey red lipstick, which caught Julia off guard with its bright hue. "She came to my gallery around half past ten yesterday and she was really worked up. She was babbling and she looked like she hadn't slept – I couldn't really understand what she was saying, but I managed to get it out of her that she had an argument with Gertrude. I tried to get some more information but she vanished as quickly as she arrived, saying she needed to go and find some money. She seemed pretty desperate."

"Money?" Julia asked. "Why would she need money?"

"She earns a good wage working at the school," Rachel said, shrugging. "But she's been acting strange for weeks. It's been getting progressively worse. We usually meet each other for lunch during the week, but she keeps missing it, saying she's forgotten, but you know Roxy, she has an elephant's memory, which is why she makes such a good teacher."

"She was the same when I saw her. She came into my café as if she didn't know where she was," Julia said, trying to steady the nerves in her voice. "I sat her down and she told me she was in trouble. Next thing I know, she had her hands on Gertrude, and then she stormed out."

Rachel clasped her hand over her mouth and closed her eyes. She stayed like that until Julia rested her hand on Rachel's shoulder. Rachel was a couple of years older than Roxy, but Julia was sure if she had been in the same class as Rachel at school, she would have been as good of friends with her as she was her sister.

"Mother called me late last night to tell me about

Gertrude," Rachel whispered when she finally dropped her hand and opened her mouth. "I jumped straight into my car and I went to Roxy's flat. She wasn't in, so I let myself in using my key. Things were all over the place and half of her clothes were missing, like she'd just packed in a hurry."

"This is worse than I thought," Julia mumbled, almost to herself. "Have you told Detective Inspector Brown any of this?"

The recognition in Rachel's eyes of the new DI's name sent a shudder down Julia's spine.

"Not yet," Rachel said. "But he stopped us both outside the church when we were coming in and asked us if he could ask some questions. Mother invited him to lunch at The Plough and he accepted."

"Don't tell him anything," Julia said. "He's looking for somebody to pin this murder on."

"So you don't think Roxy did it?" Rachel said, a frown forming between her brows.

"Do you?"

"I'm not sure. The evidence seems solid."

Julia didn't agree. Despite her nightmare the previous night, she had come to the conclusion that her friend couldn't possibly murder somebody, no matter how much trouble she was in. She knew she was missing most of the important jigsaw pieces, and she was determined to find them.

"I need to talk to Roxy first," Julia said, pulling out her ingredients notepad and a small pencil. "Do you have any idea where she might have gone?"

Rachel stared through Julia for a moment as she thought, but she shook her head and sighed.

"She's been quite friendly with Violet Mason recently. Maybe she's gone to stay with her?"

"Violet?"

"Roxy's new teaching assistant. She moved to the village a couple of months ago and she's renting a room in Amy Clark's cottage. Aside from you, Violet is the only friend my sister has."

Julia knew that to be true because she had always assumed she was Roxy's only real friend, which was why she was so surprised to hear about the existence of another. Roxy had always been very particular about who she gave her time to, something Julia had always admired, because Julia had always found herself to be too trusting. She wasn't hurt that Roxy had found somebody else to share her time with, she was glad of it, but she was hurt Roxy hadn't introduced her new friend, or at least talked about her.

She drew an arrow from Roxy's name in her

notepad and added '*Violet Mason – Amy Clark's cottage*' next to it. Rachel peered over the top of the notepad but Julia snapped it shut before she could figure out what she was writing.

"Just remembered an ingredient I need to pick up for a devil's food cake," Julia said with an awkward laugh.

Rachel narrowed her eyes, but she didn't question Julia. The two parted ways and Julia hung back to examine her notepad. She noticed she now had three names written down in connection with Gertrude's murder. She connected a line from Amy Clark's name to the main circle, wondering if wanting to take over the organ playing was a strong enough motive for murder. She decided to add a question mark next to Amy's name, but she drew a circle around Violet's because she wanted to speak to her next.

"Wouldn't be interfering in my murder investigation, would you?" Detective Inspector Brown appeared from nowhere, causing Julia to jump and snap her notepad shut. "Writing anything good?"

"Just a shopping list."

"For one of those cakes you bake?" Barker asked, displaying the smile she had come to dislike. "I hear your baked goods are quite popular in this village."

"You've been asking people about me?" Julia asked, folding her arms across her chest and holding Barker's gaze.

"All part of the investigation."

Julia didn't think Barker suspected her of murder, but she did suspect that toying with her had become his new favourite thing to do in the village. She wouldn't be surprised if he had hung back, just to make that little dig.

"I hope it's going well for you," Julia said, sidestepping, only for Barker to do the same and block her way.

"Stay away from my witnesses," Barker commanded, his tone changing from playful to serious. "I don't know what you're up to, Julie, but leave this case to the professionals."

"It's *Julia*, and I don't know what you're talking about."

"I know about the altercation between Gertrude and a Miss Roxy Carter in your business yesterday morning." Barker's smugness immediately returned. "Gertrude luckily told her son before she was murdered, meaning I want to talk to Miss Carter."

"Isn't all of that classified information?" Julia said,

pleased that she was able to match his smugness. "I don't know anything about any of that."

Barker faltered for a second but he held his stare. The amount he underestimated her radiated from his body, making her only want to find Roxy before he did even more.

"Judging from the way you were talking to her sister, I'd say you know Roxy," Barker said, glancing down at his watch as though the conversation was starting to bore him. "If you have any knowledge of her whereabouts, I'd like to know."

"Have you checked her flat?"

Barker's smug smile turned upside down in an instant. Julia knew he was trying to catch her out, but she couldn't help feeling she was already a step ahead of the man, and that pleased her.

"Classified," he said.

"Well, if you'll excuse me, I've got one of those cake things to go and bake," Julia said, stepping around Barker and walking away. "Good day, Detective Inspector."

Julia walked towards the church gates and pocketed her notepad, and without needing to turn around, she knew Barker was watching her. Instead of going to her gran's house or to her own cottage, she crossed the village green and unlocked her café door because as it happened, she did have a cake to bake. She pulled out the ingredients for an angel cake and got to work.

5

"*A*ngel cake!" Amy Clark exclaimed. "My favourite! It's so good of you to remember that, Julia!"

Amy stepped to the side and let Julia into her cottage without question. Julia had always been proud of her talent for remembering people's favourite cakes, especially in situations when she needed to use her baking skills as a form of bribery. It was a talent her mother had also shared and she used to quiz Julia on people's favourite cakes when they used to spend their Sundays baking together. She could only remember Amy mentioning that her favourite cake was an angel cake on one occasion, almost three months ago when she had visited the café and spotted a freshly baked one in the display case.

Julia handed the cake over to Amy, who hurried off to the kitchen to slice two pieces and make them a pot of tea. Julia showed herself into the living room, and even though she had never been inside Amy's cottage before, it looked exactly as she expected. Everything was either a saccharine shade of pink or blue, and all the ornaments cluttering the surfaces were animals that all had an element of cute comedy to them. Julia was assessing a figurine of a juggling cat that looked spookily like Mowgli. She tried to imagine Mowgli standing on hind legs and juggling, but the thought disturbed her; she preferred her furry friend on all four feet.

"This is as good as I remember," Amy muffled through a mouthful of cake as she hurried into the living room brandishing a tray containing a pastel pink teapot and two powder blue teacups. Julia wondered if Amy had matched her outfit to her décor, or if it had been the other way around.

They both sat on the couch and Amy poured tea into two cups. She added four cubes of sugar to her tea before passing the dish along to Julia, who opted for one.

"I just wanted to stop by and congratulate you on your excellent organ playing today," Julia said, trying to inject as much sweetness and light into her voice. "You really have a knack for it."

Amy looked genuinely taken aback by the compliment, not seeming to notice the over-enthusiastic nature of Julia's tone. Amy rested her hand on her heart and smiled pleasantly, looking on the verge of tears.

"Thank you," Amy said, nodding, as though she really were holding back tears. "You know, I was terribly nervous."

"You couldn't tell."

"I've waited all my life to get up there and perform like that," Amy sighed, and she stared off towards the comedy figurines on the mantelpiece, although she appeared to be looking through them. "It's sad that it's only under *these* circumstances that I had the chance."

The lack of remorse in Amy's voice didn't go unnoticed. She had wondered if her gran had over egged the rivalry between the two ladies, something

Dot did with most village gossip, but this time it appeared to be the truth.

"It's so sad what happened to Gertrude," Julia said, hoping to glean some information from Amy. "I still can't get the image of her out of my head. Even though I only saw the outline of her body, it's something I can't seem to shake."

Once again, Amy didn't show a flicker of emotion. She leaned forward and picked up her cup, taking a sip as though Julia had just commented on the weather. She swirled the tea around in the cup and busied herself by picking a piece of lint off of her pink cardigan.

"I imagine those things do stay with you," Amy said after what felt like an age of awkward silence. "It was surprising."

"We were all surprised."

"I think we're crossing wires here," Amy said, a strained smile contorting her lips. "I am only surprised this didn't happen sooner."

The coldness of Amy's words took Julia by surprise so much that she reached out for her tea and took a sip in hopes it would warm her. Julia stopped herself from pushing the subject further, instead choosing to divert the conversation to the topic that had brought her to Amy's sickly sweet cottage.

"Is Violet home?" Julia asked as casually as she could muster.

"Violet?" Amy tilted her head as though thinking. "I don't think so. I could check if you want? I didn't realise the two of you were friends."

"Oh, yes," Julia said enthusiastically. "Well, we have a mutual friend in Roxy Carter."

The mention of Roxy's name mustered up a reaction from Amy that Julia hadn't been expecting. She hadn't been expecting any reaction at all, so when she saw Amy's features tighten and her jaw grit, it surprised her. Amy sipped her tea through strained lips, and then forced a smile forward.

"The last I saw of Violet was when she left this morning. I was going to ask her to come to the service with me, to watch me play, but she was rather insistent that she wanted to find William Smith."

"William Smith?" Julia asked, a little puzzled.

"That's what I said," Amy said, suddenly a little more animated now that they were both back on the same page. "I told her he wouldn't want to see anybody after finding out his mother had been murdered in her own home. I suppose he's feeling guilty after their huge argument. I wouldn't be surprised if that was the last time they spoke to each other."

"Argument?"

Amy suddenly tightened up again, even more than she had at the mention of Roxy's name. Her entire body turned stiff and the teacup started to shake in her hands. Tea spilled over the edge and onto her pale blue pleated skirt. It took her a moment to react, but when she did, it felt like an overreaction.

"Silly me!" Amy cried, jumping up and setting the teacup on the tray. "What am I like?"

She hurried over to her sideboard and pulled a tissue out of the tissue box, which looked to have been wrapped in the same pink and blue floral wallpaper as the walls. She dabbed at the stain for a moment before busying herself with rearranging the figurines that were neatly placed up on it. It was obvious she was hoping Julia wouldn't push the subject further.

"What argument?" Julia repeated again.

"It's nothing," Amy said dismissively, waving her hand clutching the damp tissue. "It's probably nothing."

"Probably nothing?"

Amy sighed and returned to the sofa and sat next to Julia, but a little closer this time. She leaned in and glanced around the cottage, checking that the figurines weren't eavesdropping on their conversation.

"I was at Gertrude's cottage last night and I heard them both arguing," Amy said in a hushed tone. "He was screaming at the top of his lungs and she was just taking it. Gertrude wasn't the type of woman who would just lie down and accept defeat but she didn't bite."

"What was he saying to her?"

"I didn't hear much, I was in the other room." Amy paused and glanced around her tiny living room, before adding, "He called her selfish, I remember that much. He repeated it over and over – '*You selfish witch! You selfish witch!*' – I remember what he said just before he stormed out."

Amy stopped talking and lifted her hand up to her mouth, as though she had just realised something serious. Julia reached out a hand and rested it on Amy's knee, and she smiled appreciatively.

"Go on," Julia urged.

"He said – '*I'll make you pay for what you've done*' – and then he left."

Julia's eyes widened and her mouth suddenly became dry. She let the words sink in and replayed them over and over in her brain, as though she had heard them first hand. She thought back to last night, and wondered if the figure she had seen could have been William, Gertrude's own son, fleeing from the scene of a murder.

"Amy?" Julia said calmly, inhaling deeply.

"Yes, dear?"

"Why were you at Gertrude's house last night?"

In an instant, Julia knew her question was one too many. Amy's body tightened up again and convulsed so hard, it looked as though she was about to have a seizure from holding in her outburst so tightly.

"I really must get on with my gardening!" Amy cried, her voice shrill and cracking. "We're going to be losing the light soon and I have lots to do. Thank you for the angel cake, Julia. I'm sure I'll be enjoying that for the rest of the week. Now, if you don't mind, I'll see you out."

Julia felt the wind rush past her as the door slammed behind her. She fished out her notepad, flicked through the recipes and paused on what had become her official investigation page.

She added a single ring around Amy's name and

crossed out the question mark. Next to it, she wrote
'*William Smith*', and drew two arrows, one to Gertrude
Smith, and another to Violet Mason.

Julia suspected if she had any chance of tracking
down Roxy Carter, it was through Violet Mason.

6

*J*ulia had another night of restlessness, once again down to Gertrude, but this time over her words, rather than her death. She had stayed up for half of the night hoping they wouldn't print the damning two star review of her café, and the other half trying to figure out how to deal with the aftermath.

Standing behind her counter she let out a long yawn, and looked down at the morning's edition of *The Peridale Post*, not wanting to open it any more than she wanted to open the divorce papers still burning a hole on her kitchen counter.

As expected, the front cover and most of the inside material was filled with news of Gertrude's death. A picture of Gertrude covered the front page, but it was a picture Julia barely recognised. Not only did she look youthful and exuberant, she was smiling. There was an arm around her neck, but the rest of the picture had been cropped out. It was difficult to imagine Gertrude ever being a happy, young woman, and she wondered if that had been reality, or just a single moment captured in a photograph to paint a different picture after her death.

She selfishly skipped past the pages of tributes, and the many more pages speculating about the murder and the evidence, to the reviews section of the newspaper. She ran her finger along the page, ignoring the four star review of a local band's concert at the church hall and a new cookbook from somebody who once lived in Peridale forty years ago. When she saw the picture of her café taking up half of the bottom page, her heart sank more than it ever could.

Julia's dream to own a café was something she couldn't trace back to a single point, it was just something she always knew she had wanted to do. Baking with her mother had always been her favourite thing in the world. She died when Julia was just twelve-years-old, and everybody expected the grief to make

Julia give up baking altogether, but it had the opposite effect. She baked even more, studying her mother's old handwritten recipe books until she had them down to memory, and then tinkering with the recipes and putting her own flair on things to make them her own. She had always looked at her owning a café as a way of preserving her mother's memory and giving her a legacy.

Marrying young and moving to London derailed Julia's dream, but it never dampened. Even in her lowest lows working on a production line in a soulless baked goods factory, the glimmer of hope that she would one day do things her own way kept her going. The day she returned home to find her bags on the doorstep and the locks changed was the day she knew she had to chase that dream.

Looking down at the grainy washed out picture of her café, she felt that dream shatter for the first time in her life. All the heart she had poured in over the last two years had been sucked out in an instant, and all that was left behind were Gertrude's final bitter words about the place that painstakingly served her fresh blueberries and raspberries on her pancakes for two years. If Julia's mother's legacy was Julia's café, Gertrude's legacy was the words she had left behind.

"Morning, Julia," Johnny Watson said as he walked into the café clutching a copy of the morning paper in his hands, no doubt the first of many. "I wanted to check up on you before you got busy."

"After people read this, I doubt they'll be coming anywhere near here again."

"Don't say that," Johnny said, his soft smile comforting. "The taste buds don't lie and there's not a single person in this village who doesn't like what you bake."

"Apparently there was one." Julia pointed to the picture in the newspaper. "*Miss Piston.*"

"There'll be a new review next week and everybody will forget all about this one. Look at Rachel! Her gallery is doing fine after her scathing review last week."

Julia realised she hadn't told Johnny who the woman behind the reviews was. She almost didn't because she didn't want to prematurely turn the conversation around to what was likely to be a constant talking point for the weeks ahead, but with Dot, her sister, and Detective Inspector Brown all knowing the truth, it was bound to get out sooner or later.

"I don't think you'll be getting another review

anytime soon," she said.

"Why not?"

"Because I think '*Miss Piston*' was Gertrude Smith."

Johnny smiled for a moment, as though not knowing if she was being serious or joking, and then his brows tensed together as he pieced the jigsaw together on his own.

"*Piston!*" Johnny cried, snapping his fingers together. "Why didn't I think of that before?"

"I only figured it out right before the murder. That's why I was the one to discover Gertrude's body. I was going there to – well, I don't know what I was going to do. I certainly wasn't going to put a knife in her back, although she did the same to me, metaphorically speaking. I wanted to give her a piece of my mind, or maybe just try to reason with her, to make her see sense. I hoped if I could say the right thing, she would pull the review, or at least amend it. I shouldn't be saying any of this. It's not right to speak ill of the dead."

"Just because she's dead, it doesn't mean she's suddenly a saint," Johnny said with a smile so soft it made Julia's heart skip a beat. "Your café will survive this. You'll see."

Johnny reached out and rested his hand on Julia's, which was on top of the photograph, trying to block out all view of it. She looked down at her hand, and then quickly up at Johnny. Their eyes locked for a second, but that connection broke when the bell above the door signalled the arrival of a new customer.

Julia's relief at the interruption was short lived when she saw Barker Brown strut into her café. Johnny gathered his things, adjusted his glasses and muttered his goodbyes, his cheeks blushing all the while. For Johnny's sake, Julia wished she felt what he clearly did, but a second date was completely off the table; she loved him too much as a friend.

"Is that your boyfriend?" Barker asked smugly.

"No," Julia snapped, her own cheeks blushing. "What do you want?"

"Is that any way to speak to a paying customer?" Barker folded his arms across his chest, and scanned the chalkboard menu behind Julia's head. "More selection than I thought for such a small place. That review in the paper didn't mention your broad range of coffee and tea."

Julia felt Barker lean on the metaphorical knife that Gertrude had already planted between her shoulder blades. She had expected people to avoid her café, or even offer pity or sympathy, but she hadn't expected somebody to rub salt in the wound.

"What do you want?" Julia repeated again, not even trying to sound polite.

"It's not like you've got customers banging down the door to get in," Barker said, glancing over his shoulder to the door. "I'll have a large Americano and a scone with all the trimmings."

Detective Inspector Brown turned on his heels and chose the table under the window. Julia glanced at the clock and noticed that Gertrude should have been coming in any moment to take that seat. She had more than once stopped people from sitting there to save herself from the wrath of her most difficult customer, but now she wished she hadn't tried so hard.

Instead of rushing Barker's order, she took her time, making sure to perfectly grind and percolate the beans, not wanting the coffee to be too weak or too bitter. Even if she knew he would have some snarky comeback no matter what she served, she wanted to try and impress him. He was the type of person who could get under somebody's skin with just one look and he was well and truly under Julia's. When she ignored the obvious contempt she felt for Peridale's newest DI, the strange bubbling she felt in her stomach called out to her. It was a similar feeling she had felt when Johnny had put his hand on hers.

Pushing those childish thoughts to the back of her mind, she spooned jam and cream into one of that morning's fresh scones and carefully placed it on one of her finest plates.

When she set the order down in front of Barker, he looked up from the paper he was scribbling on. He seemed caught off guard long enough to not instantly apply his smug face, instead showing the softer version that Julia had first found so handsome, but not handsome enough to distract her from what was written on the paper. Her eyes instantly honed in on the scribbled note '*changing her will???*' in the margin.

"Working on anything important?" Julia asked.

"It's –"

"Classified," she interrupted. "Say no more."

That told Julia everything she needed to know. He quickly flipped the paper upside down so she couldn't read anymore, but she didn't need to. She was in no doubt that the papers pertained to Gertrude's murder.

With her new information, she walked as quickly

as she could while still remaining natural, and she pulled her small ingredients notepad out of her apron. She flipped it open under the counter and squinted down at it, resenting the fact that her eyesight wasn't what it had been in her twenties, and that she was probably going to need glasses soon. She pulled out her pen, flipped over the page, added a bullet point and wrote down exactly what she had seen on Barker's paper.

She muttered the three words aloud, forgetting she wasn't alone. She snapped the notepad shut and looked up, expecting Barker to be hovering over her, but he wasn't. He was still in his seat and his face was screwed up as he chewed a mouthful of his cream and jam scone. Julia allowed herself to smile because it was a face she had grown to enjoy seeing in her café. It was the face of surprised delight. Seeing Barker enjoying her scone almost made her forget about her feature in the morning paper.

Detective Inspector Brown settled his bill and left the café without saying another sarcastic word to Julia. She hoped her baking had softened his edges, but she knew he would be back to his default setting the moment the delicious fresh baked scone was a distant memory. She made a mental note to bake him something special and take it to his cottage so he could keep reminding himself that she wasn't to be underestimated. If not to impress him, then to keep him on her side so she could pry useful information from him. Even if the Detective Inspector had beaten her to a vital clue, she suspected she had more pieces of the puzzle than he had.

The rest of the day was surprisingly quiet for Julia. Out of the handful of customers she did have, only two of them mentioned the review, and they were words of encouragement, not pity. The others were more interested in her discovery of Gertrude's body, a detail that hadn't been reported in the paper, but had quickly circulated the village via different and more powerful channels. It seemed the rest of the villagers were either exhausted from their unusual trip to church, or too scared that a murderer was on the loose.

At half past five, Julia closed the café and she set off towards Gertrude's cottage, but this time she was in search of her son, William Smith.

THE ADDITION OF CRIME SCENE TAPE TO THE OUTSIDE

hadn't helped the eeriness of the cottage. The blue and white tape that had been strung across the gate had been snapped, and was fluttering wildly in the early evening breeze.

Julia looked into the cottage and unlike her previous visit, she saw a light, and it looked like it was coming from the study. There was a police car parked up the road, letting her know it was still an active crime scene, but a quick glance in the wing mirror let her know the officer was busy reading what looked to be an adult magazine.

Julia opened the gate and hurried down the garden path. She knew she was probably breaching a dozen different laws, but the door being unlocked made her feel a little less like she was breaking and entering.

As she tiptoed through the semi-dark cottage, she caught her reflection in a passing mirror and she barely recognised herself. Only last week her biggest worry had been the divorce, and now she was trying to figure out a murder case; she was sure the new DI in charge wasn't as capable as he liked to think.

Pausing outside the study where the light was emitting from, she glanced to the cottage's open front door, knowing she could turn back. The rustling of paper prickled her ears, compelling her to go forward. She pushed on the study door, which let out an almighty creak as it swung open.

A hooded shadow, much like the one she had seen in the window, was huddled over, digging through a box of paperwork. Despite the creaky hinges, the hooded figure didn't turn around, and continued to dig. Julia cast an eye around the study, avoiding the chair she had found Gertrude in. There was an obvious sign of a frantic search for something.

Inhaling deeply, Julia summoned her courage and knocked loudly on the wooden door she was standing next to.

"Hello, William," she said confidently.

The figure spun around and froze, like a police spotlight had just found them in the dark. Julia felt pleased with herself for a moment, until she saw an icy strand of blonde hair fall from under the hood.

"Who are you?" asked a woman with a heavy foreign accent.

Julia was at a loss for words, but when she finally found her voice, she realised there was only one woman the mysterious figure could be.

"Hello, Violet."

7

*V*iolet tore down her hood and stared at Julia, clutching a brown envelope in her hands.

"How do you know my name?" Violet asked, her voice dark and harsh, telling Julia that despite her youthful face, she was a woman who had lived life. "Who are you?"

"I'm a friend," Julia said, holding out her hands. "I'm a friend of Roxy's. Roxy Carter. She might have mentioned me."

Hearing Roxy's name softened Violet's expression and she dropped her hands to her sides and looked down at the envelope in her hands.

"The cake lady?" Violet asked. "I've heard lots about you."

Julia wasn't familiar with worldly dialects, but she would have placed Violet from Russia, judging by her thick, deep accent, beautiful striking features and white as snow hair. Her eyes were dazzling blue, piercing and twinkling through the dark. There was a hardness to her looks, but also an undeniable beauty and strength.

"I'm looking for Roxy," Julia said, jumping straight to the point. "Do you know where she is?"

"I was hoping to ask you the same thing," Violet said. "I have looked everywhere and I cannot find her."

Julia's stomach clenched. She believed Violet, which only condemned Roxy even more. For a moment, she dropped her guard, but she remembered where she was, and that neither of them should be there.

"Is that the will?" Julia asked.

"Will?" Violet asked, visibly confused. "I know nothing of a will. I found what I came for and now I must go."

She tried to push past Julia, but even though Julia wasn't taller than the beauty, she was wider. Julia held out her hand for the envelope but Violet moved her hand away and retreated back into the shadows, clutching it tightly to her chest.

"This does not concern you," Violet said sternly. "Let me leave."

"I don't think you understand the seriousness of what is happening here," Julia pleaded. "A woman has been murdered and I think our friend is the prime suspect. I need to find her and prove her innocence."

"Roxy would not hurt anyone."

"I don't think the police think that. She was seen on the morning of the murder arguing with Gertrude in my café. I witnessed it."

"This was separate," Violet said, clearly knowing the crucial information about what trouble Roxy was in. "I need to destroy this evidence before the police find it."

"Evidence?"

"Please, let me go." Violet's voice cracked, and Julia could tell whatever was in the envelope meant a great deal to either Roxy or Violet, or both.

Before either of them could negotiate any further, Julia heard footsteps behind her, and she felt Detective Inspector Barker Brown looming over her before she saw him.

"Well, well, well," Barker cried. "You just can't help yourself, can you Julie?"

"It's Julia," she snapped. "Pronounced Juli-*ah*."

"Of course," he said. "You're under arrest. *Both* of you."

Julia turned around to see Violet casually drop the envelope on the floor without Barker noticing. When she did, two photographs fell out of the top and it took all of Julia's energy not to gasp in shock and cover her mouth. Instead, she turned back to Barker and held her hands high enough for cuffing so that he didn't notice her kicking the photographs under the desk.

"That won't be necessary, Julia," Barker said with so much smug satisfaction, it made Julia wish she had given him one of the misshapen scones. "That is, if you're both going to come quietly?"

Both women nodded so Barker led them out of the house and towards the waiting police car outside. Julia wondered if the officer had put his magazine down long enough to spot the light in the house and call for backup. Before she could wonder any longer, Violet hopped the small garden wall and disappeared into the night. Barker started to chase her, but she was as nimble as a gymnast and vanished in seconds. Julia suppressed her pleased smile.

"Perhaps the handcuffs are necessary after all, Baker," Julia said, holding her wrists up once more.

"It's *Barker*."

"Of course."

JULIA SAT IN THE INTERVIEW ROOM AND WENT OVER HER story for the third time. She had never been arrested before, so she decided to tell Barker the truth about what had taken her to Gertrude's house once more. She told him about Amy revealing the argument, and wanting to ask William some questions about his mother's murder.

"You realise how incredibly stupid it was to visit a crime scene?" Barker said, drumming his fingers on the written statement he had taken. "You could have put yourself in danger."

"I wasn't thinking," Julia said, bowing her head.

"Who was that woman?"

"I don't know," Julia lied.

"Why do you care so much about solving this case?"

Julia stopped herself from telling him it was because she wanted to outsmart him and prove some unspoken theory that he was wrongly underestimating her, but she knew it was more than that.

"I know you suspect my friend, Roxy Carter, of murdering Gertrude, and I want to prove that she didn't."

"She's the most obvious suspect we have at this time."

"And sometimes self-raising flour is the most obvious choice for a cake but it doesn't mean it's going to give you the best results."

Barker smile at her baking analogy, but it wasn't the usual smirk, it was a softer one that was filled with an ounce more compassion than usual.

"You really love all of that baking stuff, don't you?" Barker asked, sounding genuinely interested.

"It's my life."

Julia realised how pathetic that might have sounded, but it was true. She had baking, her café, Mowgli, and her friends and family, which was why she needed to find out the truth about Roxy Carter, innocent or guilty.

"Who do you think murdered her?" The same genuine interest was present again.

"I don't think it's that simple," Julia said. "We're missing vital pieces of the recipe for the murder."

"Not everything is about baking."

"For a simple sponge cake you need flour, eggs, butter and sugar, all in equal quantities," she said, already feeling like Barker was losing his interest. "For a murder, you need a victim, a weapon, the means, and a motive."

"And a murderer," Barker added, the smugness returning.

"The cake is the result of the ingredients, as is the murderer." Julia smiled, proud of herself. "We have the victim and the weapon, Gertrude and the knife. We even have the means, that she was alone in her cottage in her study, presumably trying to change her will, from what I gathered from your notes. The only thing we don't have is the motive."

She realised what she had seen in Violet's photographs would give Roxy the perfect motive, but that was another piece of information she would keep until she spoke to Roxy.

"Since you've come this far, I might as well tell you Gertrude called her lawyer the afternoon of her

death to change her will and disinherit her son,"
Barker said without pausing for breath. "She
arranged a meeting for first thing on Monday morning, but as we know, she never made it."

"Disinherit William?" Julia mumbled almost to
herself. "Why would a mother disinherit her own
son?"

"I have no idea, but that's what I want to find out,
because I think that's the motive right there. This is
classified. You can't breathe a word of this to anyone."

"Why are you telling me this?"

Barker paused and scratched at the back of his
head. Julia was certain she noticed a slight blush
forming on his cheeks.

"Because I trust you to keep quiet," Barker said,
appearing to choose his words carefully. "You don't
seem as interested in gossip as the others."

Julia was surprisingly touched. Knowing she had
earned a pinch of Barker's trust made her chest flutter
more than she had expected. Trying not to focus on
the fluttering, she turned her thoughts to William,
and she racked her brain for everything she knew
about William, but her knowledge was sparse. She
knew he was an only child, and that his relationship
with his mother was frosty. He was a banker in the

city, but he travelled back to the village on occasion to visit his mother. She had seen him speeding past her café more than once in his sports car, with the window down and a cigarette in his hand. He had once come into her café, glanced at the menu, pulled a face, and walked straight out again. The basic information she had didn't paint a very nice picture, but did it make him a murderer?

A knock at the door derailed her train of thought and a young female constable popped her head into the interview room.

"DI, there's a visitor for Julia at the front desk," said a young female officer, sending a sympathetic smile in Julia's direction. "It's her sister, Sue."

"I'm in the middle of an interview."

"She doesn't want to see her, she just wanted me to pass this through." She produced the cake box Julia had requested her sister bring during her one phone call, and she was delighted it had made it past the front desk.

She placed the box on the table and hurried out of the interview room, leaving Barker to peel back the lid with an amused look flooding his sharp features.

"It's a double chocolate fudge cake," Julia said, peering inside at the perfect cake that had been chilling in her fridge. "I bake when I'm stressed, so I made it last night."

"And you used your one phone call to call your sister to bring it here, and not to call a lawyer?"

"Yes."

"Why?"

"I doubted you'd had much time to eat since that scone this morning," Julia said. "What with you solving a murder case and all."

They both shared a smile for a moment and for the first time, it felt like their humour was on the same page. Julia knew the effect her baking had on people, so she was glad to see it having that desired effect.

"That's very kind of you," Barker said softly. "And you're right, I haven't eaten since that scone this morning. I didn't think anything would compare."

Julia was touched by the compliment, which he delivered without a hint of irony or sarcasm. He ran his finger along the glossy icing and dropped it into his mouth.

"Wow," he said. "How did you know chocolate cake was my favourite?"

"Lucky guess."

"Did you hope you could feed me up so I would drop the charges?"

"I would never," Julia said, faking an offended gasp. "Did it work?"

"Oh, I was never going to put you through the system," Barker said with a casual shrug as he took another mouthful of the icing. "I just wanted to scare you."

"But you took a statement. You wrote four pages."

"All part of the experience. Did it work?"

"Maybe," she admitted. "A little."

"For what it's worth, I don't think you're the murderer, but I need you to promise me you're going to stay out of this investigation and leave it to the professionals."

"Okay."

"That's not the same as a promise," Barker said in a low voice, leaning across the table.

"Promise."

Her words seemed to satisfy Barker, even if her fingers were crossed under the table. She didn't like the thought that she was lying to a man she had just mentally upgraded from an enemy to an acquaintance, but if she didn't want to see Roxy behind bars, it was what she needed to do.

"Do you know anything else?" Barker asked after he finished his second slice of chocolate cake. "Any last words before I let you go?"

"That depends," Julia said. "What do I get in return?"

Barker smiled and leaned across the table.

"What do you want?" he asked darkly.

Julia leaned across the table and smiled tenderly at him for a second before saying, "Information about Amy Clark."

Barker Brown switched back to detective inspector mode, darted back in his chair, and assessed Julia from across the table. She wondered if she had undone the progress her baking had done or if he was considering what she had just said.

"I have some information on Amy Clark," he said casually, glancing over to the door. "But it depends what you've got for me."

Julia thought about the photographs, wondering if she could give the DI some useful information without putting Roxy even more in the frame.

"Check Gertrude's bank account for suspicious transactions," Julia said carefully. "I have a feeling she was blackmailing one or more villagers."

"Is this just a hunch?" he asked, his brow arching.

"Yes, but a good one. Amy Clark admitted to being at Gertrude's cottage where she overheard a conversation between William and his mother in which he called her selfish. It is common village knowledge that Amy and Gertrude are sworn enemies, so they wouldn't be meeting up for tea and biscuits."

"Is that all you're basing this on?"

"Just check," she said firmly. "Follow the money back. It might lead you to the murderer, it might not, but it's information."

Barker Brown evaluated what she had said for what felt like a lifetime as he tried to decide if what she had told him was useful or not. Julia knew there was a possibility he was going to take her information and not share what he knew about Amy Clark; she couldn't blame him if he did.

"Amy Clark has a criminal record," Barker said. "I'm only telling you this because I think it might link to what you've just told me. I had lunch with Roxy's mother and sister to try and get some information and they mentioned Amy's rivalry with Gertrude so I did a little digging and I found some pretty dark stuff from her past."

"How dark?" Julia found herself leaning in without even realising.

"Amy did twelve years in prison for assisting in a bank robbery back in the seventies." Barker said quietly. "And now that you've told me about possible blackmail, I have to consider that Gertrude knew about Amy's criminal past and was using it against her. All of this is public record, but it's a case of joining up the dots."

Julia didn't know what she had been expecting, but she hadn't been expecting something so huge. She felt a couple more of the pieces slot into place and she was happy somebody else was in Barker's mind other than Roxy.

WHEN BARKER FINALLY LET HER GO WITH ANOTHER warning to stay out of trouble, she left him alone with the double chocolate fudge cake and set off home. On her walk up the lane, she spotted a hooded figure sitting on the stone wall outside her cottage. Julia wasn't scared or surprised to see Violet there.

"You were an easy woman to track," Violet said. "Easier than Roxy. You saw the photographs?"

"I did."

"So, you know that me and Roxy are lovers?"

Violet asked, bowing her head.

"I figured that part out, yes." Julia sat on the wall next to Violet. "Was Gertrude blackmailing Roxy about those photographs?"

Violet nodded and started crying.

"That horrible woman was taking pictures of the church and Roxy was visiting her father's grave. She was upset, so I put my arms around her and I kissed her. We promised each other we would keep our relationship a secret. Roxy was so scared of a scandal at school and we were scared of losing our jobs, the one thing she loved the most. Gertrude got the pictures by accident, but the next day, she arrived at Roxy's house with them and told Roxy if she didn't pay her five hundred pounds a week, she would send the pictures to the head teacher."

"Why would she do that?" Julia mumbled, staring into the dark.

"Because she was the devil, and I'm glad she was murdered, but I promise you Julia, it wasn't me or Roxy."

"It's okay." Julia wrapped an arm around Violet's shoulder and squeezed tight. "Who you love isn't a crime."

"Even if we were a man and woman, Roxy is my

superior and my mentor," Violet said, holding back the tears. "We would both lose our jobs either way. We tried to end things, but we couldn't."

Violet started crying properly and Julia's heart broke for them both. Any sympathy she felt for the smiling, youthful version of Gertrude on the cover of *The Peridale Post* vanished in an instant.

Julia invited Violet inside for a cup of tea but she declined. They parted ways, and after Julia fed Mowgli, she crawled into bed with her notepad. She put a line through Violet's name and three question marks above Roxy's. She needed to find Roxy before it was too late.

She flipped the page and added '*blackmail*' under the note about the change of the will, along with Roxy and Amy's name in brackets. Julia would have put her savings on Gertrude blackmailing more than just the two of them.

Julia closed the notepad and rested it on her bedside table. She flicked off the lamp and slid into her soft, satin covers. The second her head rested on the pillow, she knew she was in for her best night's sleep since before the murder. Her last thought before she drifted off was if Barker had finished the rest of the chocolate cake.

8

*J*ulia was more than happy to see more of her regular customers' faces on Tuesday. She didn't realise how much she enjoyed her café being part of their lives and their routines until it wasn't. Julia had almost forgotten all about the review until she saw a copy of the newspaper clutched in Rachel Carter's hands when she came into the café during a quiet period after lunch.

Rachel pulled out a chair at the table nearest to the counter, and Julia got to work making her usual vanilla latte with an extra shot of espresso. Rachel was the only customer, so Julia took advantage of the moment and decided to take a break. She made herself a cup of peppermint and liquorice tea and sat across from Rachel.

"You too," Rachel said, pointing at the review. "I thought I'd never work again, but it turns out people in this village are rather forgiving."

"Still doesn't feel nice, does it?"

Rachel closed the newspaper and sipped her latte. Julia noticed the slight purple smudges under her eyes from lack of sleep.

"At least Gertrude can't spread more of her poison," Rachel said after taking another sip. "You're not just a master of cakes, Julia. Your coffee is the best I've ever had too."

Julia smiled and the compliment almost blind-sided her from what Rachel had just said.

"How do you know it was Gertrude?" Julia asked as she sipped her hot tea.

"I figured it out," Rachel said with a small laugh. "*Piston*? Hardly *subtle,* is it? And besides, there aren't many people in the village who were as wicked as that woman."

Julia couldn't disagree with that. After finding out that Gertrude had been blackmailing Roxy for five hundred pounds a week, Julia had run out of excuses not to agree with all of the nasty things people were saying about her. Julia knew if Gertrude hadn't been murdered, she probably would have forgiven her for the review and kept serving her pancakes, but that was the type of woman Julia was. She doubted Rachel would have been so quick to let Gertrude step foot in her gallery.

"I had an ulterior motive for coming here, aside from your excellent coffee," Rachel said, leaning in and lowering her voice. "I'm beginning to really worry about Roxy's disappearance. I can't help but think the police are trying to pin this on her, and the longer she stays away, the easier that's going to be."

"I have a feeling the police might be looking in other places at the moment."

"Oh?" Rachel seemed genuinely surprised. "Where?"

"Amy Clark and William Smith," Julia said quietly. "I think Gertrude was blackmailing Amy, and Amy swears she heard William arguing with his mother the morning of her murder. It wasn't just your sister who was on Gertrude's bad side."

"Blackmail?" Rachel asked, not sounding at all surprised. "Did you manage to find Violet?"

"I did."

"So I assume you *know*?" Rachel said, sipping her

latte again. "About the true nature of their relationship?"

"You knew?"

"Of course I knew," Rachel said, sounding a little
amused. "Roxy is my sister. She confided in me about
everything, including Gertrude blackmailing her. I
only found that out on the day of the murder. When
Roxy came to my gallery, she asked me for money,
saying Gertrude was blackmailing her, and that she
had exhausted her small pot of savings. I was quite
shocked."

Julia listened but she didn't react. She sipped her
peppermint and liquorice tea as she noticed the
sudden change in Rachel's story about that conversation. Julia could have sworn Rachel had said Roxy
was babbling incoherently when she visited the
gallery. She decided against mentioning the inconsis-
tencies.

"What time did you say you went to Roxy's
cottage?" Julia asked, diverting the conversation.

"About six," Rachel said. "Maybe a little after. It
was after I closed the gallery. Why?"

"I'm just trying to establish a timeframe. By the
time I got to the cottage, it was about six because I
remember hearing the six o'clock news. Roxy's

cottage is on the other side of the village, which means there was no way she could have gone home, packed and vanished before you got there."

"Unless she packed her things before?" Rachel added.

Julia sipped her tea again, trying not to react. Despite Rachel's worries that the police were trying to pin the murder on her sister, she didn't sound as though she fully believed her innocence.

The conversation quickly switched to idle village gossip before Rachel finished her latte and left the café, leaving behind her copy of *The Peridale Post*, which Julia tossed straight into the bin.

She was only alone in her café for less than a minute when a sports car pulled up outside, its brakes screeching as it slammed to a halt. William Smith jumped out and headed straight for Julia's café, and from the stern expression on his face, he didn't look like he wanted a cup of tea and a friendly chat.

William was a tall, slender man who looked to be in his mid-forties. He still had a thick head of hair, which was suspiciously absent of grey hairs, and his face was handsome and clean-shaven. His pale grey suit looked to be designer as did the chunky gold watch on his wrist.

"Julia South," William said coldly as he opened the door. "I want a word with you."

Julia straightened her back and put both of her hands on the counter. William's face was full of anger and rage, but Julia was determined not to match that.

"Can I help you?" she asked. "Perhaps a cake, or a nice cup of coffee?"

"You know very well I don't want a cake or a damn coffee!" William slammed his hands down on the counter. "What were you doing at my mother's cottage last night? One of the neighbours saw you being carted off into a police car, and another fleeing the scene. Your accomplice to *murder*, no doubt?"

William failed to take a breath. His face burned amber and a vein at his temple bulged violently out of his skin.

"Why don't you just and calm down?" Julia suggested. "If you want to talk to me like a reasonable adult, I'd be more than happy to."

"*Reasonable*?" He choked on the word. "You *murdered* my mother!"

"I certainly did not!" Julia cried, her tone matching his. "Now, you can sit down, or you can leave!"

William looked to the table nearest the counter

and he reluctantly sat down, making sure to make as much noise as possible. Julia had never had children, but she expected this was how teenagers acted when they didn't get their own way.

Julia sat across from him and waited for him to visibly calm down.

"I didn't kill your mother," Julia said calmly. "I went to the cottage to find you, actually. I thought you might have been there. I wouldn't have gone in, but I saw a light on, and I assumed it was you. Obviously, it wasn't you, nor was it my accomplice. I'm sorry about what has happened to your mother, but I'm trying to figure this out as much as everybody else."

William suddenly started crying, and Julia was quite taken aback. She offered him her handkerchief, which he gratefully accepted. When the blubbering finally stopped, he inhaled deeply, his face redder than ever.

"The last thing I said to her was that I hated her," William said, his voice finally calm and a reasonable volume. "If only I had known what was coming."

"None of us knew."

"I didn't have the best relationship with my mother. We never saw eye to eye on anything. I was always much closer to my father, God rest his soul."

William paused to wipe his nose with the handkerchief, and Julia made a mental note to wash it before pocketing it again. "Despite all of this, I never thought her final action in life would be to spite me."

"The change of the will?"

William nodded. He didn't bother to ask how Julia had found out.

"Now the police seem to think *I* killed her!" William cried. "It's *absurd*! We might not have liked each other, but I still loved her. I thought she loved me somewhere deep down, but this just proved she didn't."

Julia decided there and then that William hadn't killed his mother. He had been the main suspect in her mind, but seeing how fragile the man was about his relationship with his mother, she knew he could never have been the one to sink the knife into her back.

"Do you know who your mother was going to leave her inheritance to?" Julia asked.

"No. That's why I went there. She called me to let me know I was being disinherited. That was the type of woman she was. I left work, jumped in my car and drove straight there."

"And what time was that?" Julia pulled out her

recipe notepad and pencil out of her dress pocket, and flipped to the notes page.

"About five," William said. "I was gone by ten past. I knew there was no making her see sense. She had two women in her living room, and they were all drinking tea like nothing was happening. The truth is, I don't even need whatever she's leaving behind. I moved to the city and I made my own money, but it's just the biggest slap in the face."

"Two women?" Julia asked, her pencil primed over the paper.

"Yes, two," William said certainly. "One dressed in pink and blue, and one with red hair."

"How red?"

"What?"

"How red was her hair?"

"Faded," William said with a shrug. "It was greying."

Julia flipped the page to her list of suspects. She crossed out William's name and scribbled down 'Imogen Carter'. Rachel might not have inherited her mother's ginger hair, but Roxy had.

"You mentioned your father," Julia said. "When did he die?"

"Three years ago," William said heavily. "He had a

heart attack and that was it, he was gone. His wife still hasn't come to terms with it."

"Wife?" Julia asked, completely puzzled.

"My mother and father divorced in 1978," William said. "He had a lucky escape."

When Julia was alone in her café again, she scribbled down two notes. The first was '*why was Imogen Carter at Gertrude's cottage with Amy Clark?*' and the second was '*find out more about what happened in 1978*', both of which she hoped to figure out in her next visit.

After baking a box of cinnamon swirls, she set off across the village to Imogen Carter's home.

9

*I*mogen Carter's house was unusual in Peridale, in that it wasn't a cottage, and it was quite modern. Julia had always marvelled at the strange glass construction as a child, and she always loved going to Roxy's house for supper after school.

Julia remembered how much life the house had when she was a child, but now it looked sterile and cold. Imogen's husband, and Roxy and Rachel's father, Paul Carter, passed away when Roxy and Julia were teenagers, and now Imogen lived in the house alone. It looked more like a glass prison than an inviting home these days.

The doorbell rang throughout the house and Imogen Carter answered the door, with rollers in her faded ginger hair. She clutched a white silk dressing gown across her body, which looked thinner than Julia remembered.

"Julia, dear," Imogen said with a shaky smile. "So nice to see you. Come in. Do I smell the distinct scent of your cinnamon swirls?"

"The very same."

"You're an angel, Julia." Imogen beamed as she accepted the box. "I haven't been eating much, so these will go down a treat."

Julia followed Imogen across the shiny white floors of the grand entrance, which had a large domed window in the ceiling looking up at the pale blue sky above. They walked through to the living room, which was as sterile as Julia remembered. Everything was white, including the carpets, and Julia knew they wouldn't last two seconds in her cottage with Mowgli's muddy paws.

"Please, sit," Imogen offered as she tightened the tie of her silk dressing gown. "I'll make us up some tea. I have some of that peppermint and liquorice tea you like so much."

"That would be lovely."

Imogen hurried off to the kitchen, leaving Julia alone in the living room. She was scared to sit down on the white leather couch, in case the dye from her peach coloured 1940s style dress somehow leaked and injected some much needed colour onto the blank canvas.

The only colour in the entire room came from the select pictures in glass frames, which were displayed neatly on the mantelpiece, all pointing forty-five degrees to the right. Julia spotted herself with Roxy as little girls in their yellow summer school dresses. She smiled. A slightly older Rachel was in the background of the picture, pulling a face behind Roxy's back, as the two girls grinned unaware. A part of Julia yearned for those simpler days.

She heard the kettle ping and decided to sit on the couch. The leather creaked underneath her, as though it was never used, and was just for show. An opened envelope caught her attention on the gleaming glass coffee table. She recognised it as a bank statement because she was with the same bank. Julia chewed the inside of her lip and looked in the direction of the kitchen. She couldn't see Imogen, so she quickly pulled the letter from the envelope.

Julia knew she was invading her friend's mother's privacy, but she was only looking for one piece of information and she could ignore everything else.

She ran her finger down the '*PAYMENTS*' column, and snapped her fingers together when she saw a five hundred pound payment to Gertrude Smith. She heard the jingle of china cups on a metal tray, so she quickly stuffed the paper back into the envelope and sat back on the couch.

"I'm afraid I haven't heard from Roxy if that's why you're here," Imogen said as she set the tray on top of the envelope. "I'm beginning to really worry. The school even rang me to ask if I knew where she was. It's not like her to miss work. She loves that place. I hope nothing bad has happened to her."

Julia suddenly realised she hadn't even considered that Roxy could have faced the same fate as Gertrude. Her stomach turned and she pushed that thought to the back of her mind.

"I'm sure she's fine," Julia said, unsure of whom she was trying to convince. "She'll be in touch when she's ready."

"I hope so," Imogen said with a heavy sigh. "I haven't left the telephone's side. It's not like Roxy to take off and not get in touch."

Julia knew that much to be true. Roxy was the type of friend who would call, or send a text message every day of her holiday, just to let you know she was doing okay and having a fun time.

"Do you go to church every Sunday?" Julia asked.

"Church?" Imogen said with a confused smile. "Oh, not really. I was only there because the women at my book club called and said it was going to be eventful. I don't know what they were expecting to happen, but the most we got was Amy Clark's mediocre organ playing."

Julia was surprised Imogen had been the one to bring up Amy Clark because that's where she had been hoping to steer the conversation. Julia picked up her cup and took a sip of the peppermint and liquorice tea, wondering the best way to broach the subject.

"Are you friendly with Amy Clark?"

"Not really," Imogen said casually. "She's quite garish with all of that colour."

If Amy's pastel pink and blue cottage was the opposite of Gertrude's eerie dark cottage, Imogen's white and glass house was the opposite of both of them.

"So you weren't at Gertrude's house with Amy, an hour before she was murdered?" Julia asked, taking a sip of her tea.

Imogen's eyes popped open and she choked on the cinnamon swirl she had just taken a bite of. She quickly chewed and swallowed, covering her mouth with her hand.

"Where did you hear that?" Imogen asked, not denying it.

"William told me he saw two women when he went to visit his mother. I only knew Amy was there, and his description led me to you."

Imogen took a sip of her black coffee and set it back down, taking her time to adjust it so that the handle was exactly parallel to the lines of the tray. She tilted her head and observed her handiwork, as though it was the most important thing in the world.

"I was there. What of it?"

"Why were you there?"

"What business is that of yours?" Imogen snapped, revealing a different side of the woman Julia had known since childhood. "It's not a crime to visit a neighbour. I didn't kill her."

"Did your visit have something to do with Gertrude blackmailing Roxy?" Julia asked.

"What?" Imogen mumbled. "Gertrude was blackmailing Roxy as well?"

Julia frowned and tilted her head. She suddenly realised she had crossed wires.

"As well?" Julia asked. "You mean to say Gertrude was blackmailing you too?"

Imogen tried to laugh off the suggestion, but only for a split second. Her expression quickly turned grave and she pursed her lips and rested her hands on her lap. She stared sternly at Julia, and then down to the tray, as though she was seeing through it to the bank statement below it.

"Why was Gertrude blackmailing Roxy?" Imogen whispered, her eyes glazing over.

"I don't know why," Julia lied carefully, not wanting to out her friend's secret lover. "I just know that she was. Her friend, Violet, confirmed that's why Roxy has been so stressed, and I suspect that's why Roxy has gone into hiding. I also suspect she was blackmailing Amy Clark too."

"Roxy didn't kill Gertrude," Imogen said. "And neither did I!"

"How long was Gertrude blackmailing you?"

Imogen sighed and collapsed back into the couch. She rested the back of her hand against her forehead and exhaled dramatically. Whatever had been going on had clearly drained Imogen, just as much as it had

Roxy, but the mother seemed better than the daughter at hiding the truth.

"Only a couple of weeks," Imogen said after a moment's silence. "It came out of the blue. Gertrude turned up on my doorstep one night. It was quite the surprise, so I invited her in, and she said if I didn't send her five hundred pounds a week, she would –"

"Reveal your secret?" Julia finished the sentence for her.

"How do you know about the adoption?" Imogen cried, sounding more surprised than ever.

"I didn't," Julia said, suddenly putting her cup back on the table. "I just think that Gertrude knew something about Roxy and that's why she was blackmailing her, and I think she knew something about Amy, and that's why I suspect she's also a victim of Gertrude's blackmail."

Imogen sunk further into the white leather and began to sob. Julia offered her the freshly washed handkerchief, which she snatched out of Julia's hands and dabbed her eyes with.

"Nobody can know about this," Imogen said. "I don't even know how that *witch* found out. I made sure to cover my tracks perfectly. I didn't leave a trace."

"Know about what?" Julia asked, leaning forward.

"Roxy and Rachel are adopted," Imogen said with a wild sob. "Neither of them knows."

Julia clasped her hand over her mouth and her eyes widened. She didn't know what she had been expecting, but it wasn't that.

"But you and Roxy look so much alike," Julia said, unsure of why her mind went straight there.

"I got lucky with her," Imogen said, before blowing her nose on the handkerchief, which would need it's second wash of the day. "Rachel not so much. I found out very young that I couldn't have children and it was all I ever wanted. I couldn't swallow the thought of going through life not knowing the joy of being a mother. It was my late-husband's idea to adopt. I wasn't so sure because I didn't think I could love another person's child as though it were my own, but the second I held Rachel in my arms for the first time, I knew she was mine. It was a bond I had never known before. I adopted Roxy two years later and it was the same. It was so perfect, I didn't want to admit I didn't give birth to them. I didn't want anybody questioning who their real mother was, because it was me. I was raising them, so they were my babies. My husband and I swore we would never tell the girls the truth. I was going to take that secret to my grave, until Gertrude turned up that night. I was so shocked that she knew, and so devastated that she was going to tell my girls the truth, I signed the cheque there and then and I've been bank transferring the money to her since, once a week. I don't even know how she found out. She said something about not being the only one with a secret child and that's when she left."

Julia wanted to pull her notepad out to scribble down every last detail, but she stopped herself. Instead, she sat next to Imogen and pulled her into a hug. The woman sobbed for minutes without talking, before finally pulling away and drying her eyes one last time.

"You can't tell them," Imogen pleaded, clutching Julia's hands tightly. "Promise me you won't tell them."

Julia knew the girls had a right to know where they had come from, but it wasn't her place to reveal that truth to them. As she looked into Imogen's eyes, she saw desperation and heartbreak, and it was something Julia could empathise with, but hadn't experienced herself. She had always assumed she was going to have children of her own one day, but now that she was alone at thirty-seven, she knew the clock was ticking. Jerrad had convinced Julia that they should wait until later in life and she had somehow gone along with it. Looking back, she knew Jerrad had just been stalling for as long as he could until he had the guts to end things.

"I won't tell them," Julia said. "But maybe you should."

"This secret goes to the grave with Gertrude Smith," Imogen said, a strange smile filling her lips. "Nobody needs to know a thing. It's like it never happened."

Imogen resumed eating her cinnamon swirl as though nothing had actually happened. Julia left soon after that and scribbled down two new notes to her list. The first was '*Roxy and Rachel are adopted*', and the second was '*Gertrude's secret child?*'. She didn't know how either thing was connected yet, but she had a feeling they were. She flipped back to her suspects' page and drew a big arrow from Imogen to Gertrude.

10

*J*ulia pushed her peas around her plate. She wasn't particularly hungry, but her gran had gone to the effort of cooking for her, so she had tried her best to eat as much of the homemade cheese and onion pie, peas and mash as she could; it didn't help that Dot wasn't a particularly adept cook. The summons to supper had come on Julia's walk home from Imogen's immaculate prison, so after Julia ran home to feed Mowgli, she headed straight to her gran's, where Sue was already waiting for her.

"I was thinking of having my birthday party at the gallery this weekend," Sue said after sipping some of her white wine. "We could have some food, and some drinks. I could invite some girls from the hospital and we could make a real night out of it. I know I'm only turning thirty-two, but it's a reason to party. What do you think, Julia?"

"About what?" Julia mumbled.

"A party at the gallery."

Julia stared from Sue to Dot, wondering if there was something she had missed. She shook her head and dropped her fork onto the plate, and pushed it away, finally giving up on trying to force-feed herself.

"Yeah, sounds like fun," Julia said, nodding enthusiastically while also staring at the table and still deep in thought. "I'm sure Rachel will appreciate the business."

"A party is just what this village needs," Dot exclaimed. "I'll invite the girls from poker club, if that's okay with you, Sue?"

"Poker club?" Sue said with a laugh. "And that's fine by me."

"Me and some of the girls got a little bored of the weekly trips to bingo, so we meet here on Fridays and have a little tipple."

"Isn't that illegal?" Sue asked.

"Probably," Dot said, rolling her eyes heavily.

"What *isn't* these days? As long as Julia doesn't tell her new detective inspector boyfriend, we'll be okay."

"He's not my boyfriend," Julia mumbled, breaking out of her trance to look at her gran. "We barely like each other."

"Sue told me about you giving him a cake."

"I thought I was being arrested."

"He must like you if he let you off," Sue offered as she sipped her wine again. "He is rather handsome Julia, wouldn't you agree?"

"I haven't noticed," she said dismissively. "Gran, did you know Gertrude when she was married?"

Dot looked taken aback by the question. She scrunched up her face for a moment, before pushing up her tightly permed curls and nodding.

"Of course," Dot said. "I've lived in this village my whole life. The pair of them moved here when Gertrude was pregnant. You're going back some forty-odd years though. They divorced years ago."

"1978?" Julia asked.

"It must have been," Dot said with a nod. "Why the sudden interest in Gertrude's husband?"

"It's just something William said," she mumbled as she tapped a finger rhythmically against her chin. "Do you know what their marriage was like?"

"*Unhappy!*" she cried without a second thought. "She publically humiliated that man every chance she got! I'm not surprised he went looking elsewhere. He always looked so browbeaten and miserable."

"He cheated on her?"

"Old Frank?" Dot laughed. "Oh, yes! Constantly. Gertrude wouldn't admit it if you had asked her, but this village talks, and we have eyes. He was seen messing around with many women when William was a little one. He filed for divorce eventually, although Gertrude insisted she kicked him out, but nobody believed that. She was alone after that."

"Are you sure she was alone?" Julia asked.

"I'm pretty sure," Dot said. "Why is this important? Do you think it's got something to do with the murder? Last I heard, old Frank died of a heart attack a couple of years ago. You're barking up the wrong tree with that one."

Julia couldn't shake away what Imogen had said about Gertrude's secret child. It seemed important and vital to finding the murderer, but she couldn't quite piece together why.

"So there's no chance Gertrude had another child after William?" Julia asked.

Dot laughed and shook her head. Sue was staring

at Julia across the table, frowning and clearly confused. She shot her a look that said '*why do you care?*', so Julia waved her hand and turned back to their gran.

"Something like that wouldn't be kept a secret in *this* village!" Dot said. "It's impossible. She was pregnant when she arrived to the village, but never again. She had William when she was in her forties, and William was about ten-years-old when his father left, so if she had another child in her fifties, that would have been a miracle!"

The drumming of Julia's finger on her chin increased as her mind worked overtime.

"What about Frank?" Julia asked. "Did he have any children after he left Gertrude?"

"He was just as old as she was, so I don't think so," Dot said, clearly getting irritated by Julia's line of questioning. "Why is this important?"

"I haven't figured that part out yet."

"You need to let this go, sis," Sue said, reaching across the table to grab Julia's hand. "You're getting yourself into dangerous situations. I'm worrying about you."

"It's bigger than me," Julia said. "There's a

murderer on the loose and if I don't find them, who will?"

"The police?" Sue said, laughing as though it was an obvious statement. "Detective Inspector Brown?"

"He doesn't see the bigger picture." Julia sighed. "He's a typical man. Thanks for dinner, Gran, but I should get home. It's been a long day and I have baking prep to do for the morning."

"But I have trifle in the fridge!" Dot cried. "You can't go yet!"

Julia knew the trifle would have been store bought. Her gran was her father's mother, so the baking gene was on the other side of the family, not that it had passed to Sue. Sue was okay when it came to measuring and putting things in the oven, but she lacked Julia's finesse and skills to bake truly delicious treats.

After taking her plate through to the kitchen, Julia slid into her pink pea coat, kissed her gran and sister on their cheeks, and headed out. She inhaled the night air, appreciating the slight chill. She hoped the walk home would unlock something vital in her brain. She felt like she had all the pieces of the puzzle and the sooner she put the pieces in the right order, the sooner she could get back to worrying about baking, instead of the murder.

Julia put her hands in her pockets and looked in the direction of her café. Even in the dark, it filled her with pride. She tried to imagine the life she had had back in London, but it felt like it belonged to somebody else, which only made her wonder why she was so reluctant to sign the divorce papers sitting in her kitchen. She didn't want Jerrad, nor did she really want him to suffer. The relationship with the secretary he had left her for hadn't lasted longer than six months and he had gone through two other women since. He was welcome to that life, she just couldn't help feeling he had taken the easy way out, and she had been forced to start her life all over again. She was grateful for that now, but a little part of her, the part that was stopping her from signing the papers, wanted to put a little obstacle in the way of what Jerrad wanted.

Her thoughts snapped right back to reality when she noticed movement in her café. She thought it was her imagination, or the dark playing tricks on her, so she hurried across the village green. When she saw the definite outline of somebody emptying the contents of her display case, she knew she was witnessing her mystery cake thief in action.

Julia turned back to her gran's cottage, and then to the local police station up the road, but she decided she was going to confront the thief alone.

Instead of going for the front door, she crept along the alley where she usually parked her blue Ford Anglia, and to the small stone yard behind her café. She saw the beam of a flashlight moving around behind the counter as she carefully stepped into the kitchen. Being as careful as possible, she closed and locked the back door.

Julia crept to the beaded curtain separating it from the front of her café. She peered through the beads and watched a tiny, slender figure chomping down on a slice of her latest addition, the lemon sponge cake that she had perfected over the weekend.

"Enjoying that?" Julia asked.

The figure spun around, and to Julia's surprise, she was greeted by a teenage girl. She dropped the cake and scooped up her bag, but she seemed frozen to the spot. The girl looked from Julia to the front door, assessing her exit route.

"It's okay, you're not in trouble," Julia said softly when she saw how alive the fear was in the girl's eyes.

"Why don't you sit down and I'll cook you something proper?"

The girl raised an eyebrow and glared at her as though she was mad, but to her surprise, she slowly walked around the counter and sat in one of the seats, not taking her eyes away from Julia. After flicking on some of the lights, Julia left the girl sitting in the chair and staring around the café, and she went into the kitchen to see what she could throw together. The only other food she served other than her cakes were toast and pancakes, so she put as many slices of bread into the toaster as she could, and set herself to making scrambled eggs with some of her cake ingredients.

She set the food in front of the girl, who under the light looked like she needed a good wash. The girl looked down at the food and up to Julia before she grabbed a slice of bread, scooped up as much of the eggs as possible and crammed it into her mouth. Despite the knife and fork Julia had placed next to her, she repeated the grabbing and scooping with her dirty fingers and black nails until the plate was empty. It was obvious she hadn't had a decent meal in a while.

"What's your name?" Julia asked when she sat across from the girl.

The cake thief looked to the beaded curtain and Julia knew she was considering her escape, but she turned to Julia and looked down her nose at her, as though deciding she was going to toy with Julia.

"What's it to you, lady?" the girl asked.

"How can we have a conversation if I don't know your name?" she replied, offering a soft smile. "I'm Julia."

Julia held her hand out, even though the girl's fingers were dirty and now covered in butter and egg grease. The girl stared down at their fingers before slapping her hand into them.

"Jessika with a *k*," she said proudly. "Everyone calls me Jessie."

"Well, Jessie," Julia said as she discreetly wiped her fingers on the edge of her dress under the counter. "Do you mind telling me what you're doing in my café, and how you got in here?"

Jessie stared at Julia through narrow slits, as though she was trying to figure out if Julia was a woman to be trusted or not. Julia pushed forward her friendliest smile, and Jessie smiled back a little.

"You should really get a good security system,"

Jessie said looking around the café. "The back door is too easy to pick. You're lucky it's me and not some of the others."

"Others?"

"Homeless folk," Jessie said, as though it were obvious. "They're not all honest people like me."

"Honest people don't break into people's cafés and steal."

"It's not stealing if it's food," Jessie said. "Not really. I just really like your cakes, lady."

Julia was touched by the compliment.

"How old are you, Jessie?"

"Old enough," she snapped back.

Julia chuckled. She liked Jessie's spirit. It didn't seem that Jessie was going to give Julia that information, so Julia had to guess for herself. She had dark hair and pale skin, which was covered under a layer of grime and dirt. If Julia had to guess, she would have guessed the girl wasn't any older than eighteen.

"Why are you homeless, Jessie?" Julia asked.

"Because I am."

"Don't you have parents?"

"Dead." Jessie said in a matter-of-fact voice. "Died when I was a baby. Been in the system ever since."

"So you ran away from a care home?"

"Foster parents," Jessie said, and Julia sensed a hint of anger deep in her voice. "They're not even looking for me. Been gone for three months."

"I'm sure they are looking for you."

"They're not, lady," Jessie snapped. "They just care about the money. Got some more of that new lemon cake stuff? It's good."

Julia smiled and nodded. She went into the kitchen and pulled the cake out of her fridge. She cut a slice bigger than she had ever cut before and took it through to Jessie, who was scratching furiously as the back of her thick, unwashed hair.

Jessie devoured the cake in record time, even licking her fingers afterwards. Julia knew she couldn't sit by and let this child go back out into the world in such a state, so she came up with a plan in that moment.

"How would you like to come to my cottage and shower? I'll even give you a bed for the night, if you want to take it."

Jessie stopped licking her fingers and scowled at Julia. She stared down her nose again, her eyes scrunched up as she thought about what Julia had just offered.

"What's the catch?" Jessie asked, folding her arms across her chest. "There's *always* a catch."

"No catch." Julia held up her hands and sat back at the table. "That's the offer. Take it or leave it."

Jessie wrinkled up her face again, but it seemed the offer of a hot shower and a bed was too much to pass up. She shrugged and picked up her bag, and waited for Julia to lead the way.

After locking up the café, they walked up to Julia's cottage in silence. Jessie jumped at every small sound, making Julia wonder how many nights the poor girl had spent outside alone. Had she slept rough through the long winter?

Jessie spent almost an hour in the shower, emptying Julia's boiler out of every last drop of hot water. She didn't mind. When she walked past the bathroom to see if Jessie was okay, she heard her singing a song Julia recognised off the radio, and it put a smile on her face.

After her shower, she sat in front of the fire, which Julia had got going just for her guest. With a towel tucked under her armpits and another in her hair, she sat shivering in front of the flames. Without the layer of grime on the girl's face, she looked even younger than Julia had first thought.

"Why are you being nice to me?" Jessie asked out of the blue, jolting Julia from reading her Gertrude notes over and over.

"Everybody deserves kindness," Julia said.

Jessie smiled and bowed her head. She bid Julia goodnight and headed off to the guest bedroom Julia had made up for her. If Sue or Dot found out about her houseguest, they would think she was irresponsible for letting a homeless thief into her home. If it had been another person, Julia might have agreed, but she saw Jessie for what she was; a lost girl who enjoyed her cakes and needed an ounce of compassion.

Mowgli curled up in her lap as she sipped her fresh peppermint and liquorice tea. When she heard loud snoring coming from the guest bedroom, she pulled out her laptop and balanced it on the chair arm, and for the first time since the murder, she researched something other than Gertrude Smith.

11

*W*hen Julia popped her head into the guest bedroom on Wednesday morning, she wasn't surprised to see Jessie had already left. The bed had been perfectly made, and the towels had been neatly folded at the end of the bed. She wondered if she would ever see Jessie again, or if that was the end of her stolen-cake mystery. Now that Julia knew the truth, she wasn't sure if she was happy she had cracked the case.

On the other hand, she was eager to crack the murder case. A good night's sleep had reenergised her efforts to find the killer, and she had woken up with a possible theory about Gertrude's secret child.

Julia pulled the red velvet cake out of the oven

and placed it straight onto the cooling rack. Mowgli ran in from the garden, his fur covered in dandelion spores. He shook them off before jumping up onto the counter to pad towards her, adding more muddy paw prints to the already covered divorce papers.

"What do you think, Mowgli?" Julia asked as she stroked under his chin. "Do you think I'm being silly by not signing this and getting it over with?"

Mowgli purred and bounced up to butt her face. Julia wanted to believe her cat was telling her she should open and sign the papers in her own time, but she knew he was just hungry.

After feeding Mowgli, and icing the red velvet cake with butter roux icing, she hopped into her blue Ford Anglia and set off towards the village. She only travelled a couple of metres before Emily Burns jumped out into the road waving her arms. Julia slammed her foot on the brakes, and they screeched out, stopping inches away from Emily. She didn't seem to notice how close she had come to being hit because she scurried around to Julia's door and waited for her to roll down her window.

"Have you heard the news?" Emily asked as she pulled her gardening gloves off. "William Smith has been *murdered*!"

"*Murdered*?" Julia gasped, her hand drifting up to her mouth. "Are you sure?"

"I've had *four* people call me already this morning to tell me!"

Julia knew the Peridale gossip network could spread false information in a heartbeat, but she doubted something so serious would make its way around the village so quickly if it weren't true.

"I need to go," Julia said, winding her window up before Emily could engage in conversation.

She sped down the winding lane faster than she had ever driven before. As she passed Barker's cottage, she slammed on her brakes again when she saw him pushing his arms into his camel coloured trench coat, a slice of burnt toast clenched between his teeth.

"Is it true?" Julia asked as she jumped out of her car. "That William has been murdered?"

"Good morning to you too, Julia," Barker mumbled through the toast before tossing it into the grass and wiping the butter and crumbs from his lips with the back of his hand. "Where did you hear that?"

"Is it true, or not?"

Barker unclipped his gate and walked around Julia and towards his car.

"It's true what they say about small villages," Barker muttered under his breath, a dry smile already forming on his lips. "I only just found out myself and yet the gossips are already talking. Yes, it's true."

The smile quickly dropped when he seemed to remember that the gossip in question was about a dead man.

"Was he stabbed, like his mother?" Julia asked.

"That's need-to-know information."

"If somebody found his body, that information will be all around the village in no time, if it isn't already."

"That's just it," Barker said as he ducked into his car. "One of our officers was walking home past the village green when they saw Amy Clark leaning over the body, soaked in William's blood."

Detective Inspector Brown slammed his car door. Julia knocked on the window until he wound it down.

"You've arrested Amy Clark for William's murder?" Julia asked.

"Not just his murder, Gertrude's too. You were right to be suspicious of Amy Clark," Barker said as he twisted his key in the ignition. "You've done your part, Julia. Get to your café and carry on with your life. I'm sure you'll have plenty of customers today who all want to use your business as a gossip hub."

With that, the window slid up and Barker sped off down the winding lane, taking the corners dangerously sharp.

THE ENTIRE DRIVE TO THE CAFÉ, JULIA WAS TRYING TO understand why she didn't feel relieved that somebody was in custody for both murders. Amy Clark had been one of her prime suspects. She had the means, the motive, and the opportunity, and she had been caught red handed at the scene of a second murder, but something didn't sit right with Julia. She wondered if it was because it felt like an anti-climax to her investigation. Had she really expected to walk into the station with her little notepad, having figured out the murder? It felt like something that would wipe the smile off Barker's face, but she knew it wasn't realistic.

Julia drove past the village green and her heart sank. A crime scene tent had been erected in the middle of the green, and crime scene tape had been wrapped around it. Men in white body suits came and went as the early risers of the village stood around the edges, whispering amongst themselves. She spotted her gran in the mix of villagers, but she was so deep in her gossiping that she didn't notice Julia's unique car driving by.

Even though she hated to admit it, Detective Inspector Brown was right. Now that the murderer was behind bars, she could get back to focusing on her café. The double murder would give Peridale plenty to talk about for months to come, but she knew the village would move on and get back to normal eventually.

Julia pulled up at the opening of the small alley between her café and the post office where she always parked her car, but despite the 'STRICTLY NO PARKING' sign on the side of her café, there was already a car there. Sighing, Julia killed the engine and jumped out, hoping the driver was still inside. As she walked to the car, she quickly recognised it as William Smith's sports car.

Turning to look at the white tent, she wondered if William had parked his car here before walking to his death. The thought turned her stomach. The police hadn't seemed to notice the victim's car parked in the shadow of her café. She considered calling the station right away, but she couldn't resist a peek of her own through the tinted windows.

Careful not to touch anything, Julia cupped her hands as close to the window as she could, and peered inside. It was a typical man's car, covered in old food wrappers from motorway service stations, and old newspapers. She spotted that week's copy of *The Peridale Post* on the floor of the passenger seat, underneath a sausage roll wrapper. In the cup holder, there were two white coffee cups from a chain coffee shop, which naturally made Julia's hairs stand on end. She didn't know how anybody could drink such over-processed, over-sweetened nonsense. Red lipstick on the rim of one of the cups caught Julia's attention. She thought she recognised the shade as belonging to somebody in particular, but she wasn't sure if she was over thinking things.

Using her black cardigan to stop the transference of her fingerprints, she tested the handle, and to her surprise, the car door was unlocked. It seemed that when William parked, he didn't think he would be away from his car for very long. It upset Julia that he hadn't known he was walking to his death. She hadn't known much about the man, nor had she really liked him, but after seeing him cry about his emotionally unavailable mother, she couldn't help but feel saddened that he had succumbed to the same fate.

Julia ducked into the car to get a closer look at the cup. Without the tint of the windows, she unmistakably knew she had seen that particular orangey shade of red lipstick before, because only one woman had features so striking to pull it off. She also picked up on the distinct whiff of a badly made vanilla latte. Using her cardigan again, Julia ripped off the cardboard lipstick print and pocketed it, vowing to hand it over to the police after she had gone to talk to the owner of the fresh print.

After leaving a hastily written '*back in twenty minutes*' sign in the café window, she jumped back in her car and drove across the village to the art gallery, and when she saw it was closed, she redirected to Rachel Carter's cottage.

12

Rachel Carter's cottage was similar to Julia's, in that it was on its own winding lane leading out of the village. The cottage was traditional on the outside, with its low roof, small windows, and old stone, but the inside showed that Rachel had inherited her mother's tastes for minimal, clean living.

"Julia!" Rachel exclaimed when she opened the door. "I was about to call you."

"You were?" Julia said as she stepped into Rachel's cottage. "I can't stay long, I haven't opened the café yet. I just wanted to ask you a question."

"So you're not here about Roxy?" Rachel asked, her eyes narrowing.

"Roxy?"

"She turned up this morning," Rachel said. "She's in my guest bedroom sleeping. She was in quite a state."

Julia followed Rachel down the hallway to the guest bedroom, where Roxy was fast asleep on top of the bed. Her skin was pale and she looked frailer than Julia had ever seen her look before. Julia's initial feelings of relief were quickly replaced with more sinister ones. She had so many questions she wanted to ask Roxy, but she couldn't justify waking her up. She didn't know where she had been since Saturday, but it didn't look like she had been relaxing in a spa.

"I suppose you've heard about William?" Julia asked, already pulling the lipstick printed piece of cardboard out of her pocket.

"Mother called at the crack of dawn," Rachel said as she led Julia through to the sitting room. "Quite sad."

Despite Rachel's declaration of sadness, she didn't appear at all to be sad. Julia would have gone as far as to say that Rachel seemed rather indifferent to the news. She wondered if she had jumped to conclusions about the lipstick. Rachel was wearing the same orange tinted red she had worn to church on Sunday, but Julia knew it wasn't impossible that somebody else in the village would own the same shade, or even somebody outside the village.

"Your lipstick is nice," Julia said.

"Thank you," Rachel said with a smile. "Roxy bought it for my birthday. I wasn't sure if it would suit me, but people seem to like it. It's quite unique."

"Did you know much about William?" Julia asked, quickly redirecting the conversation.

"No more than the usual," Rachel said suspiciously, her eyes tightening. "The flash car, job in the city. Did you come here to ask me about William Smith? If so, it's a wasted journey. What's that you've got in your hand?"

Julia looked down at the lipstick print and suddenly wondered if she had taken herself on a fool's errand. Her gut had told her to ask Rachel about it, so she decided that's just what she was going to do. When her gut told her a cake recipe needed a touch more butter, or a dash of cinnamon, it was rarely wrong.

"I found this in William's car," Julia said, handing the piece of cardboard over. "It is parked in the alley next to my café and the door was open. I recognised it as the shade you wear. Like you said, it's unique."

Rachel accepted the piece of cardboard, her expression barely flickering. She held it up to the light for a moment, before tossing it onto the clutter-free glass coffee table, crossing one leg over the other and resting her hands on her knee.

"It's mine," Rachel said sternly.

Julia was taken aback by the quick admittance.

"Do you know how it came to be in William's car?"

"Of course I know," Rachel said with a small laugh. "Because I was in his car. Listen, Julia, I might as well be honest with you, not that it's *any* of your business. William and I have been seeing each other romantically. It was never serious and it was never going to be. He came into the gallery a couple of months ago to buy a painting, and we went out for coffee after. When he came back to the village, we met up. Ever since his mother's death, his moods have been frantic, and it was becoming exhausting, so I asked him to meet me late last night. He picked me up after the gallery closed and he drove me to one of those awful motorway service stations. Nobody can make vanilla lattes like you can. I broke it off and then he dropped me off, and that was the last I heard from him."

"Have you told any of this to the police?" Julia asked, picking up the torn piece of cardboard. "You were one of the last people to see him alive."

"It's not important," Rachel said. "I don't know why he hung around in the village. Our relationship was nothing more than a fling. It meant nothing to either of us. He wasn't even bothered when I told him we should call it off. In fact, he agreed it was probably for the best."

Julia thought back to the blubbering mess she had comforted in her café and wondered if that same man would have been okay with any slight rejection. She wasn't so sure.

Before she could ask more questions, Roxy skulked into the sitting room, rubbing her red raw eyes. When she spotted Julia, she immediately burst into tears and wrapped her arms around her neck.

"I've been so worried about you," Julia whispered into Roxy's ear. "Where have you been?"

"I've been so stupid, Julia," Roxy said, sobbing against her shoulder. "So stupid."

When Roxy calmed down, they sat next to each other on the sofa. Once again, Julia wondered if her friend could be capable of murder, and she was surprised when she couldn't come to a definitive answer.

"Where have you been?" Julia repeated. "Why did you leave the village after Gertrude's murder?"

"Oh, Julia," Roxy sobbed into a tissue. "I had no idea Gertrude had been murdered. I ran away because of – *because of* -"

Roxy's voice trailed off and she continued to heavily sob.

"I know about the blackmail," Julia said. "I know about Violet too. The *truth* about you and Violet. I've met her and she told me everything."

"She did?" Roxy peaked up through the soaked, almost shredded tissue, glancing awkwardly to Rachel. "That's the reason I left. I couldn't stand the thought of ruining her career as well as my own. That morning before I came to the café, Gertrude came to my home, demanding more money than ever. She wanted one thousand pounds as a final payment, and she would leave me alone. I didn't have *that* kind of money! I teach six-year-old children for a living. She'd emptied my savings and I was desperate. I hadn't been sleeping and I felt completely lost. I thought about asking my mother for the money, but I knew that would mean telling her everything, and I couldn't bring myself to do that. When I left the café, I went home and packed my things. I jumped on a train and I went to stay with an old friend from university, Beth. I've been sleeping on her sofa, trying to figure out my next move. I knew I needed to get as far away from Peridale as I could, that way Gertrude couldn't find me. I thought maybe she would forget about the final payment if I weren't around to remind her. I thought if I left Peridale, Violet would be safe. She would keep her job, and everything would work out okay for her. It's silly really. I wasn't *thinking*. I had barely slept a wink for weeks."

"Why did you come back today?" Julia asked, a hard lump rising in her throat.

Roxy wiped away the last of her tears and she sat up straight. She brushed her considerably faded red hair out of her face and turned to look Julia dead in the eyes. Julia wondered if she was looking into the eyes of a killer.

"Beth was on the computer, reading the news. She saw an appeal from the police asking for information about a murder in Peridale. She called me over and I read all about Gertrude, and how she had been stabbed, and that they were looking for me for questioning. I got on the first train back, and I came straight here. I was going to go straight to the police, to explain that I wasn't even in the village when Gertrude died, but I crashed out."

"So you don't know about William Smith?" Julia asked softly. "Gertrude's son?"

Roxy frowned, her eyes narrowing to slits. She opened and closed her mouth, but she didn't make a sound.

"He's been murdered, Roxy," Rachel said. "Stabbed like his mother."

"What?" Roxy said, shaking her head. "*No, no, no*! I didn't do it, Julia, *I swear*! I know what it looks like, but I didn't do it!"

"It's okay," Julia said. "They've arrested Amy Clark."

"Amy Clark? The church lady?" Roxy asked, looking just as confused. "Why would she do such a thing?"

"Gertrude was blackmailing her too," Julia said. "It's a long story, but you don't have to worry. Just stay here. Don't leave Peridale again. Just *stay* here."

Julia stood up to leave, but Roxy grabbed her hand and dragged her back down to the sofa.

"Don't leave me," Roxy pleaded. "Please."

"I need to," Julia said with a soft smile, prying Roxy's fingers off of her hand. "I'm going to go speak with Amy."

Julia kissed Roxy on the cheek and headed towards the door. Rachel followed her, softly closing the door to the sitting room.

"Are you going to tell Detective Inspector Brown about my relationship with William?" Rachel asked quietly as they hovered near the front door.

"I think it's important he knows, if only to establish a timeline before his death."

Rachel nodded, considering what Julia had said, before applying a small smile.

"I understand," Rachel said. "It's better he hears it from me. If you're driving to the station, can I ride with you?"

"What about Roxy?"

"She'll be okay," Rachel said, glancing back to the sitting room door. "She'll probably just fall asleep again. By the way, your sister called last night about having her birthday party at the gallery tomorrow night."

And just like that, the conversation switched from murder to birthday parties. When Rachel started talking about balloon colours and bunting, Julia tuned out, and instead turned her thoughts to how she was going to convince Detective Inspector Brown to let her talk to a suspected murderer.

13

*P*eridale police station was a tiny place. It usually dealt with petty crime and local squabbles between neighbours, not double murder cases. From the moment Julia stepped inside and asked to speak to Detective Inspector Brown, she could tell the station's resources were being stretched to capacity.

While Julia waited for Barker to make an appearance, Rachel spoke to the officer behind the front desk. After a minute, he instructed Rachel to take a seat, but instead of sitting next to Julia, she sat on the opposite side of the station's waiting room and busied herself with reading a magazine.

"Julia, whatever it is, I don't have time for it," Barker huffed as he marched towards her.

"I need to speak to Amy Clark," Julia said. "It's urgent."

As expected, Barker laughed at her, his head shaking heavily.

"*Impossible!*" Barker cried. "She's currently being interrogated about these murders. I've got my boss breathing down my neck to solve this double murder. I thought I was moving to this village for an easier life, but this is more complicated than any case I've worked in my entire policing career."

"I don't think Amy did it," Julia whispered, standing up so that she was level with Barker. "If I can just speak to her, I think she can tell me something that will point us straight to the real murderer."

Barker stared down at her, as though trying to decide whether he should laugh or cry. Julia held her stance and darkened her stare, to let him know she was being deadly serious. Just when he was about to say something, an officer ran towards him and pushed a piece of paper into Barker's hand.

"*Dammit!*" he cried, screwing the paper up in his hands. "Her alibi checks out."

"Alibi?" Julia asked.

"She said she was shopping at a supermarket outside the village. I didn't believe her but the supermarket has confirmed that she was seen on the security cameras and was spotted by several members of staff at the time of the murder. Who travels out of town at five in the morning to go shopping?"

"A woman who doesn't want her fellow villagers to know she doesn't shop locally because she prefers the choice and price of the chain supermarkets," Julia said calmly. "Please Barker, all I need is five minutes with her."

AMY LOOKED EQUALLY CONFUSED AND RELIEVED TO SEE Julia when she walked into the investigation room. Barker sat on a chair in the corner and motioned for Julia to sit across from Amy, who was clutching a weak looking plastic cup of tea in her shaking hands.

"I didn't do it," Amy whispered as she sipped her tea. "Oh, Julia, I *didn't* do it."

"I know," Julia said soothingly. "I believe you. I think you can help me figure out who did though."

"I don't know anything!" Amy cried as she pulled her powder pink cardigan together. "I was just driving home from the supermarket when my headlights caught the poor man's white shirt on the village green. The sun had only just started to rise, and I thought he was a drunk, so I got out and told him what for. When he didn't move, I walked over and that's when I saw the knife, and that it was William. *Oh, Julia! It was awful!* The poor man was still alive. I held him and I screamed out for help, and that's when the officer found me. I know how it looks, but I swear to God, I didn't kill that poor boy."

Julia wanted to tell Amy that her alibi had cleared, but Barker had made her swear not to. She wondered if he still suspected her and that she would confess with a little more pressure. Julia knew they could interrogate her for the next ten years and she would never confess.

"I know Gertrude was blackmailing you about your past," Julia said. "You weren't the only one. She was also blackmailing Imogen and Roxy Carter."

"I knew about Imogen," Amy said, a frown forming in her crinkled brow. "But why Roxy?"

"That's not important right now," Julia said. "You have known Gertrude for a long time, haven't you Amy?"

Amy sighed and nodded.

"Can you believe we used to be friends? When I –
when I – oh, you know the truth about my past. When
I was released from prison, I knew I wanted a fresh
start away from anybody who knew me as Amelia
Clarkson. I was born Amy Clark, but that was the
name I went by when I -"

"Robbed banks?" Barker jumped in.

Amy shot him daggers across the room before
turning back to Julia.

"Those were the days," Amy said with a soft sigh.
"I know it wasn't right, but I haven't felt as alive as I
did when we were on a job. It's almost as though it
happened to another woman in another life, but
those memories are what keep me warm at night. My
mother said I got in with a bad crowd, but I was the
leader of that crowd. I deserved every year in prison
that I served, and I wouldn't change a second of it. I
found God when I was in prison. I used to play the
organ at the Sunday service. When I moved to Peridale, that's what me and Gertrude bonded over. We
were thick as thieves for the longest time, until I
found out she was blocking me from ever playing the
organ at service. It was Father Wentworth back then,
and Gertrude had him wrapped around her little
finger. I always thought she had an eye for him, but

she would never be unfaithful to her Frank, even if he didn't pay her the same courtesy. She wouldn't let me play the organ just once. Not *one* time. She could *never* share. We went from being friends to enemies and that's how it stayed. When she died, all I could think was '*it's my time to shine.*' I asked God to forgive me for even thinking that, but Gertrude got what was coming to her."

Julia almost felt bad for always viewing Amy Clark as the old lady who liked to wear colours associated with newborn babies. She had seemed like an old lady for as long as Julia had known her, and Julia had never even considered that she had lived a life before that.

"Did Gertrude have any other children after William?"

"Gertrude?" Amy laughed. "*Impossible*! By the time Frank left, she was already too old. Why do you think that?"

"I don't, I was just checking to make sure my theory was correct," Julia said, glancing over to Barker, who was sitting on the edge of his seat staring curiously at her. "What about Frank? Is there any way he got one of the women he was having an affair with pregnant?"

"One of the women?" Amy said with an amused smile. "There was only ever one. Martha Tyler. She was Gertrude's only friend, but Gertrude treated her as badly as she treated Frank. She was younger and prettier than Gertrude. She must have noticed her husband had an eye for another woman. Martha and Frank fell madly in love. Martha confided in me that she was going to run away with Frank and start a new life. I *encouraged* it. I saw how Gertrude treated Frank. Their marriage had been dead for years before the divorce. Separate bedrooms, you know what I'm saying. Gertrude couldn't handle being left for another woman, even if she had caused it herself, so she spread the rumour that Frank had been cheating on her with multiple women. That became the truth. It was easier to admit that he had been unfaithful, rather than admit that he had fallen in love with somebody who appreciated him."

"So Frank and Martha married?" Julia asked.

"That's the strange thing," Amy said, tapping her finger against her chin. "They never made it down the aisle. Before they ran away with each other, Martha called things off and vanished. Frank was devastated but he didn't stay with Gertrude. He left Peridale and he eventually met somebody else. I never met Frank's new wife, but he seemed happy. He would fill me in on details of his new life with his annual Christmas cards, but they trailed off eventually. I didn't see him again until his open casket at his funeral. I feel like I'm the only one left from the old gang."

"And Martha?" Julia urged. "What happened to her?"

"That's another strange thing," Amy said, looking off wistfully into the corner of the room. "About a month ago, Martha turned up in Peridale. She visited me at my cottage and it was as though no time had passed. She even looked the same, just older. Her hair was as black as it had always been. I was always so jealous of it. She told me she was dying, and she wanted to make peace with the village before she left. She died a week later and I went to the funeral, but I didn't recognise anybody there. I asked Gertrude if she wanted to come, but she refused to even say Martha's name, so I went alone. The blackmail started the day after the funeral."

Julia's mind buzzed, and the theory her dreams had pushed forward had only been strengthened with Amy's new information.

"Well, that was useless," Barker said as he walked

her back through the station. "Just an old lady reminiscing about the good old days."

"Yes," Julia agreed, biting her tongue. "Will she be released?"

"We've got twenty-four hours to charge her, but with that alibi, it doesn't look like we can. Is there anything else I can do for you, or can I get back to my job?"

"There's one thing, actually," Julia said. "If I wanted to see if a person had been reported missing, how would I go about that?"

"You want to report a missing person?" Barker asked.

"No, I want to see if somebody else has," Julia said as she reached into her handbag to pull out her notepad. "A girl in her late teens."

She ripped off the page where she had written down everything she knew about Jessie.

"Is this connected to the case?" Barker asked as he skim read the information.

"No, but it's important to me," Julia said. "Is there anything you can do?"

Barker folded the small piece of paper and pocketed it, giving Julia his word that he would check the missing persons database and get back to her with what he found.

"By the way, William Smith's car is parked in my space next to the café," Julia said as she left. "You might want to get somebody to move it."

JULIA QUICKLY DROVE HOME, LEAVING HER CAR OUTSIDE her cottage. She hurried down to her café, which had been closed an hour after opening time. A small crowd had gathered outside, and they cheered when Julia pushed through them to unlock the door. She told them a lie about waking up late and quickly fastened her apron around her waist, and got to work.

When her sister appeared during a quiet period after the lunchtime rush to pick up a vanilla slice and a cappuccino, Julia pulled her into the kitchen.

"I need three blank invitations for your birthday party tomorrow night," Julia whispered quickly. "I'm going to need them to figure out who killed Gertrude and William Smith."

*a*fter work on Thursday, Julia put a box of cakes, along with a blanket and a note for Jessie in the stone yard behind her café. On Friday morning, she was happy to see that her café hadn't been broken into and the box, blanket and note were gone.

A little after opening, Barker entered, her first customer of the day. He ordered a shot of espresso and two slices of toast and sat at the table nearest the counter.

"Amy Clark was released last night," Barker said as he tucked into his golden buttery toast. "Back to square one."

"Not quite square one," Julia said, hovering

behind the counter and focusing on wiping away something that wasn't there. "Did you find anything about the missing girl?"

"Jessie?" Barker mumbled through a mouthful of toast as he pulled a folded sheet of paper from his pocket. "Or should I say, Jessika Rice. Sixteen years old, been in the care system her whole life. She has a criminal record longer than my arm. Breaking and entering, theft, resisting arrest, breaching the peace, you name it, this girl has done it. She was reported missing after disappearing from her thirteenth foster home, taking two hundred quid with her on the way. She sounds like a piece of work."

Julia took the paper from Barker and scanned over it. She wasn't too bothered about the long list of crimes, but she was happy to see that Jessie had been honest about her name. That told Julia more about the girl, who she couldn't believe was only sixteen, than any files on a computer would.

"Thank you, Detective Inspector," Julia said, slipping the paper into the pocket of her pale yellow dress. "I really appreciate it."

"Friend of yours?"

"Not yet."

Barker tossed back his espresso, licked the butter

from his fingers, and left. He gave Julia another vague warning of staying out of trouble, to which she waved her hand. Julia wasn't alone for long before Roxy walked into the café, looking much better than the last time Julia had seen her.

"On the house," Julia said as she set a latte and a chocolate brownie in front of her.

Roxy smiled appreciatively and took a bite of the brownie. She closed her eyes and licked the chocolate from her lips, as what looked like intense pleasure washed across her face.

"I thought I would never taste your brownies again," Roxy said. "I don't know what I was thinking running away."

"Have you spoken to the police?"

"The new DI came around this morning," Roxy said. "Brown, or something. Quite handsome. Have you met him?"

"I have," Julia said, wondering if there was anybody in the village who didn't find Barker handsome. "Have you spoken to Violet yet?"

"Only on the phone. I'm going to see her next, but I needed some caffeine for courage. I don't even know where to begin apologising to her, for dragging her into this, and then running away. All it took was a good night's sleep to see how foolish I was."

Julia pulled two of the three envelopes from her pocket and placed them next to Roxy's plate.

"Invitations to Sue's birthday party tonight," Julia said. "One for you, and one for Violet."

"I'm not sure I'm up to it," Roxy said, assessing the invitations with caution. "Rachel told me about it, but I don't know if I can show my face."

"The sooner you do, the sooner people will get the gossiping out of their systems and move on," Julia said. "Besides, it's a good place to debut your new relationship. It's better to do it now while there's plenty of other gossip floating around. People will hardly notice."

Roxy thanked her and pocketed the invitations. Julia hurried back into her kitchen, exhaling a huge sigh of relief that her plan was working. She pulled out her notepad and flipped to the list of notes she had made last night. She crossed off Roxy and Violet's names and circled Imogen's, having already decided she wanted to drop that invitation off herself.

∾

JULIA SPENT THE REST OF THE DAY RUSHED OFF HER feet struggling to keep up with the amount of customers coming through the door. News of Sue's party had spread, and the people with invitations were expressing their excitement, and the people without were either asking Julia for permission, or inviting themselves. Julia knew the gallery could hold as many people that were going to turn up, and if her plan worked, the more people in the village to witness things, the better. She didn't want there to be any wiggle room on the facts when it was all over.

Julia pulled up outside of Imogen's white and glass house, and peered through the windows. She could see Imogen sat in her silk dressing gown, watching television. Julia wondered if word of the party had spread this far out into the village yet.

With her invitation in hand, Julia walked up to the house and pressed the doorbell. When Imogen answered the door, she looked less pleased to see Julia than the last time she had been there.

"I hope this won't take long," Imogen said. "My show is about to start."

"I just wanted to drop this by," Julia said, passing Imogen the envelope. "An invitation to Sue's birthday party tonight. I know it's short notice, but I know she would love to see you there."

"*Tonight*?" Imogen said with a wrinkle of her nose as she brushed her fading red hair out of her face. "I'm not sure I'm very much up to it, Julia. I heard Roxy was back, but she hasn't been in touch. Sometimes I wonder if those girls know the truth about where they came from. They've been growing further and further away from me recently."

"I'm sure they're just busy with everything else that has been going on," Julia said reassuringly. "Roxy told me herself she wanted to see you at the party."

Julia felt bad telling a white lie, but Imogen's face lit up. She looked down at her dressing gown and sighed heavily, before tossing her head back and nodding.

"Fine!" Imogen cried, waving her hands. "But I need to start getting ready right *this* minute if I'm going to be anywhere near presentable for the party!"

JULIA LEFT IMOGEN TO PAMPER HERSELF, AND SHE WENT back to her own cottage and did the same. She changed out of her pale yellow dress, which was full of coffee stains and flour, and she slipped into a simple black dress, in her usual flared 1940s style. She spent more time than usual sorting her hair out, creating a victory roll in the front and pinning the curls up in the back. Berry red lipstick, black mascara, and rose-tinted blusher completed the look, along with her mother's understated diamond earrings and necklace; the only things Julia had inherited, aside from her baking skills.

After slipping into some uncomfortable black heels that Sue had bought her two years ago, she stepped in front of the floor length mirror, which she usually rushed by in the mornings, her appearance being the least of her worries.

Julia caught herself off guard. She barely recognised the woman staring back at her. Gone was the café owner who loved to bake, and in walked a striking woman. Everybody always said Julia looked like her mother's twin. She had never seen it much herself, until she was looking at herself done up in the mirror. The last time she had put this much effort in to her appearance had been Sue's wedding, almost ten years ago.

Pleased with her efforts, Julia hurried downstairs, fed Mowgli, and headed for the door. On her drive down the winding lane towards the village, she spotted Detective Inspector Brown sitting on a rusty, wrought iron bench under his living room window reading some papers. To her surprise, he looked up when he heard her car's old rattling engine, and he stood up. Julia slowed down and pulled up next to his car.

"Julia, you look -" Barker mumbled as she got out of the car. "New dress?"

"Just something I had in the back of the wardrobe," she said. "Nice tuxedo."

"Your sister invited me to her birthday party tonight, so I thought I would make an effort."

"She did?" Julia said through almost gritted teeth.

"She was quite insistent."

"That's my sister, alright," Julia said, wondering why she hadn't seen her sister's meddling coming. "Reading anything interesting?"

"Case notes," he said regretfully. "Trying to see if there's anything I've missed, but it's all just a blur. Half of me wants to stay in tonight and go over everything, but I know the break will give my brain a chance to recharge, and it will be a good chance to meet some more of the locals."

Julia thought back to the man who had arrived in

Peridale almost a week ago, and she couldn't imagine that same man having any interest in meeting the local residents. It seemed more than just Julia's double chocolate fudge cake that had softened his edges. Even with the double murder case to contest with, she knew not many could resist being sucked into village life.

"Well, I'll see you there," Julia said, turning back to her car. "I promised Sue I would help put the finishing touches to the party."

"Want to go together?" Barker asked suddenly. "If I stay here, I'll only keep reading the same sentence I've been reading for the past twenty minutes, plus, knotting balloons is a special talent. We'll take my car. I don't trust the look of yours."

"There's nothing wrong with my Ford Anglia!" Julia said, stroking the bonnet. "She's vintage."

"She's *something*."

Barker pulled his keys out of his pocket and unlocked his car. Julia picked up a pile of paperwork on top of the seat and tossed it into the back. As she did, the file flipped open, and her eyes honed in on the police report made by Rachel Carter yesterday at the station. Something in the first sentence caught her eye, so she grabbed it and screwed it up into her fist before Barker saw.

With the paper clenched tightly in her fist, they drove to the gallery, and Barker's side-glances to her didn't go unnoticed. She was glad she was wearing makeup, or he might have noticed her face burning up as she concealed a smile.

15

*I*t turned out Julia and Barker weren't needed at all to help get things ready for the party. When they walked into the gallery, everything was as it should be. Sue and her husband, Neil, were sipping champagne, along with Dot. They all turned and spotted Julia at the same time, and she detected their eyes widening when they noticed who she was accompanied by.

"This place looks amazing," Julia said as she looked around at the bunting and balloons decorating the white spaces between the art. "You've done a really lovely job."

"I took the day off work," Sue said as she leaned in for a kiss. "You look amazing, Julia."

"Doesn't Julia look beautiful, Detective Inspector?" Dot asked, casting her champagne flute in Julia's direction.

Julia wanted the ground to swallow her up, and she could feel Barker wishing the same. Her gran was many things, but subtle wasn't one of them.

"She does," Barker agreed, scratching at the side of his head. "Any more of that champagne?"

"This way, mate," Neil said, wrapping his arm around Barker's shoulders. "You like football?"

Neil and Barker walked off towards the food and drink table, leaving Julia with her sister and gran. She fixed her attention on an abstract painting of what she thought was St. Peter's Church from the village, hoping they wouldn't interrogate her.

"Tell me *everything!*" Sue squealed. "I knew you two would hit it off! I *knew* it!"

"Thanks for the heads up on his invite," Julia whispered. "And there's *nothing* to tell. I was driving past his cottage and he suggested we take the same car. I thought you would need an extra pair of hands to help with the decorations."

Sue rolled her eyes, clearly not believing Julia. Even Julia wasn't sure if she believed herself. She glanced over to Barker, and the flutter in her stomach was too strong to be ignored.

"I never thought he could look more handsome, but that tuxedo has proved me wrong," Dot whispered, before sipping her champagne.

"I hadn't noticed," Julia said, hearing the lie in her voice. "How long before people arrive?"

"About fifteen minutes?" Sue checked. "Gran, why don't you go and grab Julia some champagne?"

Dot tutted as she turned on her heels to shuffle off towards the men. Rachel appeared from her office with a phone crammed against her ear. She waved and smiled to Julia as she headed for the front door.

"So," Sue urged. "Did you get your invitations out?"

"I did."

"And you know who the murderer is?"

"I think so."

"You only *think* so?" Sue whispered desperately. "I gave you permission to ruin my birthday party on the one condition that you were sure."

"I found something earlier," Julia said, pulling the screwed up piece of paper from her handbag, making sure Barker wasn't looking over. "A police report Rachel Carter filed about William Smith. She told me they were having a secret affair, so I told her to tell the police. I don't even think she realises it, but she's pointed me to the murderer in the first line of her statement."

Julia smoothed the paper out against her dress and handed it to her sister. She read over the first couple of lines, her brow furrowing.

"*But -*"

"Yes," Julia jumped in.

"So that means -"

"It does."

"Are you going to -"

"Tell Detective Inspector Brown?" Julia took back the paper and folded it up as small as it would go before stuffing it back into her bag. "Why ruin the fun? Either way, he'll have his murderer in jail and I -"

"Will have proven Barker wrong," Sue jumped in, finishing Julia's sentence for her. "If you didn't like him, you wouldn't care so much about proving yourself."

"I need you to do something for me later on."

"Is it legal?" Sue asked suspiciously. "You've been getting up to all sorts recently."

Julia told her what she wanted her to do, but before she even agreed to helping with Julia's plan, the first guests arrived and Sue rushed off to greet them. Dot returned with champagne for Julia, and a small plate of buffet food that she had taken from under the foil covered plates.

"Tonight's going to be a long night," Dot mumbled through a sausage roll. "You know how I hate parties."

"I'm sure tonight will be a night to remember, Gran," Julia said softly before sipping her champagne. "You'll see."

AN HOUR INTO THE PARTY, JULIA WORRIED HER invitations hadn't worked. Just when she was about to call Roxy to check up on her, she walked in hand-in-hand with Violet, with Imogen trailing behind. The befuddled look on Imogen's face told Julia that Roxy had told her the true nature of her relationship with Violet. People immediately started to stare and whisper, but neither Roxy nor Violet seemed affected.

"You made it," Julia said as she walked across to them. "You all look beautiful."

"Blimey, Julia!" Roxy cried. "I almost didn't recognise you."

Roxy was wearing a floor length, red satin dress, which beautifully complimented what looked like freshly dyed red hair. Imogen was wearing a body-hugging white wrap dress, which cut off just above the knee. Her faded hair had been curled and pinned back, and she had a white shawl wrapped around her arms. Violet was the one who had undergone the most dramatic transformation. When Julia had seen her under the black hood, she had known she was beautiful, but she hadn't realised how beautiful she really was. Violet's icy blonde hair was slicked back off her face, giving her striking features room to shine. She had opted for a floor-length glittering silver dress, which was low-cut in the front, and had a slit running from the bottom of her right foot, all the way up to the hip. She looked as though she had been pulled from the pages of a high fashion magazine, and Julia doubted Peridale had ever seen anything like it.

"It's nice to see you again, Julia," Violet said, her accent as thick as Julia remembered. "You look very beautiful."

"Nothing compared to you," Julia said, blushing under her makeup. "But thank you."

"Where are the drinks?" Imogen muttered, then

headed off to the table at the back before Julia had a chance to answer.

"She's still processing it," Roxy said when they were alone. "I think she's mourning the loss of ever having any grandchildren. What with Rachel turning thirty-nine and still being single, I think she had her hopes pinned on me finding a nice man, and instead -"

"You found me." Violet beamed, kissing Roxy on the cheek. "We will give her grandchildren, don't you worry about that."

Julia left them alone. She was happy for them, but their new love reminded her of how things had been when she had first met Jerrad. He had promised her their love would last a lifetime, and that he would give her everything she wanted, including children. Julia tossed back her champagne, wondering why she had believed a man like him.

"Good party," Barker said when they met at the buffet. "I was right about the night off reenergising me. I feel ready to come at this case with fresh eyes tomorrow."

"I'm sure you'll find the murderer in no time," Julia said as she tossed a strawberry into her mouth.

"Is that Amy Clark?" Barker whispered, squinting into the crowd. "That woman has some nerve."

Julia turned to see Amy Clark making her way through the crowd, which parted like the Red Sea around her. She shuffled forward sheepishly, and when she caught Julia's eye, she headed straight for her. It didn't matter that Amy Clark had been released, news of her arrest would have travelled around the town, and an arrest was as good as guilty in most people's eyes.

"I knew I shouldn't have come," Amy whispered as she brushed down the front of her pink and blue dress. "I should go."

"Life is too short to miss out on parties," Julia said as she handed a glass of champagne to Amy. "Enjoy yourself. People will get bored soon."

"Are you sure about that?" Amy asked with a nervous laugh. "I'm sure people will know about my past soon, and then I'll be chased out of the village."

Julia couldn't imagine anybody chasing a lady in her eighties out of the village, but she knew how scary the thought of being the subject of the villagers' gossip could be. She had experienced that first hand.

"The only people who know about that are you, me, and Detective Inspector Brown, and we're not going to tell anybody, are we?" Julia said, staring up at Barker with a raised eyebrow, who stared down at her confused, so she gave him a swift and sharp kick in the shin with her heel.

"No, we won't," Barker said. "You deserve a second chance."

Amy thanked them both and joined the line of people queuing at the buffet. Julia wasn't very hungry, so she ditched the plate of food she had gathered up. She and Barker walked out to the garden behind the gallery. Twinkling lanterns shone brightly against the ebony sky, sending a warm glow over the beautiful flowers. They sat on a bench at the bottom of the garden, enjoying the silence for a moment, listening to the chatter and the music as it floated out from the gallery.

"I misjudged this village," Barker said after ditching his food. "It's not what I had expected."

"Why did you come here in the first place?" Julia asked.

"I was bored of the city," Barker said with a soft smile. "Bored of the same crimes. I wanted a change of pace. When the idea of transferring to a small village came up, I took it with both hands."

"And you got two murders in your first week."

"What a welcome that was." Barker chuckled softly. "It's unlike any place I've ever been before. Despite everything that's happened, the people here are full of so much life. My last birthday, four people turned up to my party, and they were all from work. Everybody in the village has come to celebrate with your sister."

"I think most of them have come to see if there's any news about the murders," Julia said. "If gossiping was an Olympic sport, Peridale would take gold."

"I've noticed that. Makes my job difficult. Half of the village know things before I do."

Julia thought about all of the things she knew that she still hadn't told Barker. For a moment, she felt guilty for withholding the information, but she knew if she revealed everything she had figured out to the detective inspector, he might dismiss some parts as trivial and focus on the wrong thing. If everything went to plan, all of the dirty laundry would be out in the open before the night was over.

"I think you'll do just fine here, Detective Inspector," Julia said with a smile. "It can take a while to adjust from the city, but you'll be part of the furniture in no time."

"You've lived in a city?"

"I spent twelve years of my life away from this village," Julia said heavily. "Worst decision of my life."

"Well, I'm glad you're here now," Barker said.

Julia turned to look at him, and their eyes locked, as did their smiles. If it hadn't been for the look in Barker's eyes, she might have taken his comments as throwaway. She didn't notice she was leaning in to kiss him until her eyes closed. Through her lids, she felt the detective inspector doing the same, but before their lips met, a sneeze cracked through the silence like a whip.

Julia pulled away as quickly as she had leaned in, to see her gran tiptoeing across the grass.

"Hay fever," Dot mumbled apologetically.

"I should be -" Barker whispered.

"We were just -" Julia added.

Dot smiled and turned on her heels. She shuffled back into the gallery, chattering to herself, no doubt exclaiming what a good couple they would make. Julia turned to Barker, sure that her makeup wasn't hiding her embarrassment this time. Neither of them spoke, instead choosing to awkwardly laugh. They headed back into the gallery in silence and quickly split up.

Julia caught Rachel talking with her mother, so she moved in closer and joined their conversation.

"Have you seen Roxy?" Imogen asked. "I feel like I've been saying that a lot recently. I don't know what's got into that girl."

"I haven't," Julia said. "Maybe she and Violet have gone out for some air?"

Imogen pursed her lips at the mention of Violet's name, which she followed up with a heavy roll of her eyes. She walked away, leaving Julia and Rachel alone.

"She'll get over it eventually," Rachel said. "She's from a different generation."

"Love is love," Julia said. "They look more in love than I ever was with my husband. Have you ever been in love, Rachel?"

"Do you mean with William?" Rachel chuckled. "It wasn't love, it was just a casual thing."

Before Julia could delve more into Rachel's relationship with William Smith, Sue hurried over, visibly out of breath.

"Something's happened in the other room," Sue panted through short breaths. "I think you need to come and see this, Rachel."

Rachel looked from Sue to Julia, clearly panicked.

They both followed Sue into the other gallery, which was separated by a door labelled *'closed for the party'*. From her previous visit to the gallery, Julia knew the second room in the gallery contained some of the more valuable works Rachel had on display. The second they walked in, it was apparent what had happened, even though the lights were dimmed to almost darkness. The biggest painting in the centre of the main wall had been slashed right down the middle.

"The Georgia O'Keefe!" Rachel cried, clutching her hand over her mouth. "Who could have done this?"

Julia looked desperately to her sister, who shrugged.

"I came in here to make a phone call away from the noise and I just found it like this," Sue said quietly. "I'm so sorry, Rachel. Was it valuable?"

"Priceless," Rachel whispered, her voice choking. "I studied Georgia O'Keefe at university, and this was the crown jewel in my collection."

Julia turned her head to look at the two halves of the slashed painting. She knew Georgia O'Keefe painted flowers, but she was struggling to see the beauty in the art. She was more accustomed to seeing the beauty in her baking.

"I'm calling the police," Rachel said as she reached into her bag to pull out her phone. "This isn't acceptable. This is worse than murder!"

Julia eyed to Sue to leave them alone, so Sue hurried back to the door, her heels clicking on the wood flooring. When they were alone, Rachel hugged the phone to her chest as she ran her fingers along the frayed edge of the canvas.

"It's not even a clean cut," she whispered. "It's beyond repair."

"Are you sure?"

"I'm positive," Rachel said. "I don't understand why somebody would do this."

Julia glanced around the empty gallery as she reached into her pocket for the paper. She pulled it out and unfolded it, her hands shaking. Rachel turned around and looked down at the paper in Julia's hands, but she was far enough away that she wouldn't be able to read it in the low light.

"When you made your statement to the police about your relationship with William did you tell them everything you told me?" Julia asked, keeping her voice low so the rest of the party wouldn't hear them.

"Excuse me?" Rachel said, her face screwing up. "What does that have to do with my painting being ruined?"

"Nothing," Julia said, passing the paper over to Rachel. "I just didn't expect Sue to go to such extremes when I asked her to come up with a reason to get you in this room so that I could follow you in."

Rachel looked at Julia and then down at the paper. She read through it expressionless before tossing it. Julia watched the paper flutter down to the floor, the slither of moonlight shining in through the tall windows casting its shadows into the darkest corners of the room. It hit the floor weightlessly, but Julia was sure she heard it crack through the hefty silence.

"You just can't help yourself, can you Julia?" Rachel's features suddenly darkened as she reached into her handbag to pull out something shiny and silver. "You should have stuck to baking."

Julia stared down at the knife and was surprised by the sudden lack of fear. She was so overwhelmed with the amazement that her theory had been correct, it blinded every other basic human emotion, but she suspected looking into the eyes of a killer would do that to a person.

"How long have you known you were adopted?" Julia asked calmly, not taking her eyes away from the shimmering blade, which seemed to be growing with every second. "Is it the same time you found out that Gertrude's ex-husband, Frank, was your real father, and that William was your half-brother?"

Rachel slowly clapped her hands together, the knife blurring from side to side. She dropped her hand and let out a low, chilling laugh.

"You figured out *all* of that from my false police report?" Rachel said, glancing down to the report she had made, claiming that somebody had stolen her mobile phone. "Aren't you a clever one, Julia South? I always thought you were wasted in that café."

Julia spun around as Rachel circled her, the knife swaying from side to side. Taking a moment to compose her thoughts, Julia blinked slowly before taking a step back from Rachel.

"Amy Clark told me Martha Tyler came to Peridale to find peace with the village she once called home, but I think she came to find somebody she had said goodbye to thirty-nine years ago. Martha had been having an affair with Frank Smith, and I don't doubt that she loved him, but I think Gertrude discovered that Martha was pregnant before Frank did, and she scared Martha away. Of course, I don't know for certain that Martha was pregnant, but it's the only thing that makes sense to me, the only thing strong enough to tear people apart and force them into making bad decisions. I suspect Gertrude knew something life changing about Martha, and she used it against her to drive her husband's pregnant mistress out of the village, in hopes of saving her marriage. Of course, it didn't work, and Frank married somebody else, leaving Martha to raise a baby on her own. Maybe it was too much for her to be a single parent, or maybe she couldn't stomach the thought of raising Frank's baby on her own, so she gave the baby up for adoption. That baby was you. I figured that out when Amy Clark mentioned Martha's black hair, I was just trying to figure out if you were really capable of murder. Just as Imogen and Paul Carter were looking to adopt their first child, you were brought back to Peridale. How ironic that Gertrude wanted to get rid of you, but you came back here. I would say it was a cruel twist of fate. I doubt Gertrude figured out who you were until Martha tracked you down and told you her secret before she died. I suppose it came as a shock to you that you were adopted, and you were looking for somebody to blame, and Gertrude was that woman."

"She denied me ever knowing my real parents!" Rachel cried, tears welling up in her eyes. "My real mother and father could have been a part of my life if it wasn't for that witch!"

"After you found out the truth about your birth, you went to Gertrude and I think you blackmailed her."

"I wanted to make her pay!" Rachel said with a dark laugh. "She *deserved* to *suffer!*"

"Little did you know, in order for Gertrude to pay you, she used the secrets of your own family to black-mail them in return. She was lining your pockets with money from your sister and mother, but I suspect you didn't know that at first. Of course, you were clever enough to keep all of the blackmail out of the banks, so nothing would ever be traced back to you."

"It wasn't until she wrote that nasty review of my gallery in *The Peridale Post* that I found out. She thought she could ruin my business and run me out of town, but it only made me angrier. I went to her cottage, saw the pictures of Roxy and Violet, and she told me about the blackmail. I found out the truth when I met Martha, so when I found out she was also blackmailing Imogen I put the pieces together, so I went to confront her. She said she was going to disinherit William and leave everything to me. She said she felt guilty about what she had done. *Ha*! I didn't believe her. I spent a little time with my real mother, but it was too late. It wasn't enough to make up for those lost thirty-nine years. She thought I would blame her, but I didn't. There was only *one* woman I blamed. I panicked, so I picked up a knife and I drove it into her back. It was the only thing I could do! Her money didn't make up for what she had done to me. I always knew I didn't fit in, but I found out far too late in life to do anything about it. She robbed me of a life I should have had! Gertrude told Martha that Frank knew about the pregnancy, and that he didn't want anything to do with the baby. She believed her and left. Frank never found out about me because of Gertrude."

"You never had a secret affair with William," Julia said. "Instead, you killed your half-brother."

"He was going to go to the police!" Rachel cried, shaking the knife in Julia's face. "He called the lawyers and his mother had been stupid enough to give them my name over the phone! They wouldn't tell the police, but because William was the heir to Gertrude's estate, they revealed the nature of the phone call. When he confronted me, he suspected that I had some information on his mother. I was blackmailing her, and that's why she was black-mailing people herself. He was so furious, so I told him the truth. At first, he was happy to find out he had a half-sister. He told me he had always resented being an only child. Resented that his mother had waited so late in life to have him, and yet here I was the whole time. William told me his dad, Frank, had always wanted a daughter too. What good was that information to me? It was all *too* late. His happiness didn't last long when he figured out what I had done. He wouldn't listen. He got out of the car and started walking to the police station, so I did what I *had* to do."

"You murdered your half-brother in the middle of the village green and you let Amy Clark take the blame."

"Nobody saw me!" Rachel said, almost pleased with herself. "And Roxy was at home to be my alibi. I was there when she arrived and fell asleep, and if the police ever suspected me, she'd tell them I was there when she woke up. Everything fell into place perfectly. Even you didn't notice it was me when you saw me at Gertrude's house! You almost caught me, so I smashed the window and made a run for it. I went to Roxy's house instead, and I saw that she had gone. By then, I knew the truth about Roxy's lover, but I knew nobody else did, so if she had run away, it would make her look guilty."

Julia was speechless. She stared at Rachel, a woman she had known since childhood, but she didn't recognise her. She had always been a little distant and cold, but she had never suspected she would be capable of murder, or willing to let her own sister take the blame.

"You're sick," Julia said.

"Oh, shut up, Julia!" Rachel yelled, raising the knife above her head. "You always were a little know-it-all!"

She struck the knife down, but Julia grabbed Rachel's wrist. They wrestled for what felt like an age, and the blade floated dangerously close to Julia's face. She expected to see her life flash before her eyes, but she didn't. Instead, she felt an intense feeling of survival she had not experienced before. She was suddenly reminded of all the things she had to live for, and she wanted to live for them. She needed to live.

"You would have let them arrest me?" Roxy's voice floated around the corner of the gallery, her lipstick smudged and her hair messy. "Rachel, I can't believe what you've done."

Rachel turned and watched Roxy and Violet walk towards them from the shadows, just long enough for Julia to knock the knife out of Rachel's hand with her handbag. She turned to Julia, but Julia wasn't going to take any chances. With strength she didn't know she possessed, she pushed Rachel into the wall and brought the slashed Georgia O'Keefe painting down around her body.

"Get Detective Inspector Brown!" Julia told Violet as she kicked the knife away. "*Hurry!*"

16

The entire party crowded outside the gallery and watched as Detective Inspector Brown escorted Rachel towards the flashing lights of the police car. Julia was surprised by how she wasn't putting up a fight.

Julia couldn't begin to imagine what it would feel like finding out you were adopted after thinking you knew where you came from for thirty-nine years. She could imagine how resentful Rachel had felt towards the woman whose meddling had caused her to live a lie, but she couldn't imagine that feeling ever driving her to murder. She couldn't imagine Gertrude knowing she had signed her own death certificate decades ago with her desperate attempts at saving her broken marriage.

"I'm sorry you had to find out like this," Julia whispered to Roxy. "If I'd have known you were there -"

"If I wasn't there she would have killed you," Roxy said, wrapping her fingers around Julia's. "I had missed Violet so much, so we broke away from the party to – *you know*. I would like to say that I always knew I was adopted deep down, but I didn't. My mother and father are the people who raised me, not two strangers who created me. I don't know why Rachel couldn't see that. How did you figure out it was Rachel, and not me?"

"Rachel told me that you told her about Violet when you went to visit her the morning of the murder, but I figured out that you probably didn't visit her at all."

"I didn't," Roxy said. "How did you know that?"

"When I went to Rachel's cottage to ask her about the lipstick, you talked about the blackmail and running away, but you never once mentioned that Violet was your lover. You were being very conscious about your words, so I suspected that Rachel had found out about the relationship from another source, and there was only one woman in the village who knew."

"Gertrude!"

"Exactly."

"I don't know what to say," Roxy said with a heavy sigh. "My own sister would have watched me go to prison."

"I would never have let it get to that," Julia whispered, pulling Roxy into a hug. "I figured this out to stop that from happening."

When Roxy finally let go, she thanked Julia and walked towards her mother, who was sobbing on the edge of the road, while being comforted by Violet. Despite everything, Julia knew they were going to be okay.

"How did you piece it together, Julia?" Amy Clark asked loudly enough to grab the attention of the watching crowd, who all turned their attention from the police car to Julia.

"It all came down to the lipstick," Julia said. "I saw a lipstick stain on a coffee cup in William Smith's car and I knew the unique shade belonged to Rachel. Gertrude and Frank divorced in 1978, so when I suspected Martha Tyler had a secret baby, and that Martha had been in Peridale a month ago, I knew the murderer had to be that baby, and had to be somebody who was thirty-nine. Looking back, Rachel was the only person I spoke to who never denied killing Gertrude or William."

"But why would she do such a horrific thing?" Dot asked as she glared at the police car as it drove away.

"She was just a lost girl who didn't feel like she fit in," Julia said. "Gertrude symbolised that pain, and William just got in the way."

An hour later, Julia was standing behind her counter in the café with most of the village crammed into the tiny space. Her till was filled with what she suspected to be record takings, and the place was bursting with more life than the busiest Saturday at the height of summer. Gertrude's two-star review was already a distant memory.

The bell above the door rang out and another person wrestled their way through the thick crowd to the counter. Julia smiled when she saw it was Barker.

"Can I have a word?" He said, his expression stern.

Julia took him through the beaded curtain to the kitchen, and she leaned against the steel counter in the middle.

"Next time you have vital information about a murder case, I'd appreciate it if you told me before you approach the suspect," Barker said, his tone firm, but his eyes and smile soft. "You could have got yourself killed."

"I was fine."

"I'm being serious, Julia," he said, shaking his head as he paced in front of her. "When I found out she had a knife, my heart sank. She wouldn't have hesitated to make it a third murder."

Julia knew he was right, but she was touched that he seemed to care more about her wellbeing than she did. In that moment, she had been running on adrenaline, but it had taken multiple sugary teas in the café to calm her nerves.

"How is she doing?" Julia asked.

"She's currently confessing to everything," Barker said, and he stopped pacing and leaned against the counter next to her. "How were you so certain it was her? Rachel Carter wasn't even on my radar! I was trying to find an accomplice of Amy Clark. I was *so sure* she had something to do with it."

"I wasn't completely certain until I approached her, but this was the final nail in the coffin," Julia said as she pulled Rachel's police report from her dress. "I stole this from your car. When I came to speak to Amy Clark yesterday, Rachel came with me because she told me she had been having a secret affair with William Smith. I found evidence that she had been in his car, and she claimed to have broken things off hours before he was murdered. When I saw the police report in that file on your passenger seat, and I saw that she had reported a stolen mobile phone, I knew she had lied to me. On the surface, she seemed like the only person without a motive, but Amy Clark's story allowed me to piece history together to figure out what happened in the present. You heard the same information as I did in that interview, but sometimes it takes a close ear to the ground and a finger on the pulse of the village to really *listen* to the information you're being told."

Barker turned to her and for a moment he looked angry, but his expression softened and he smiled, their eyes locking like they had in the gallery's garden.

"I really underestimated you, Julia," Barker said.

"You did something I couldn't do myself. You ignored the obvious and you listened to people's stories."

Hearing what Julia had wanted to hear all along didn't fill her with the same happiness she had expected. She realised she hadn't just been trying to prove Barker wrong about her, but to prove him wrong about the village she loved so much. For that, she felt she had succeeded.

"Did you just come here to tell me off?" Julia asked, glancing back through the curtain at the busy café.

"Actually, there was something else," Barker said, sucking the air through his teeth. "How would you like to grab a coffee sometime?"

"Coffee?" Julia asked. "I own a café."

Barker dropped his head and laughed softly.

"I'm trying to ask you out on a date, Julia," he said quietly, his cheeks flushing.

"Oh, I know," Julia said.

"So?"

"I'll think about it."

"You'll think about it?" Barker said, arching a brow. "Is that all I get?"

"Yes," Julia said, nodding sternly. "I'll think about it."

Barker pushed the air out of his lungs and shook his head once more. He smiled at Julia and nodded, before turning on his heels and walking back through the curtain. When she was alone, Julia allowed herself a moment to let the grin spread from ear to ear. She intended to go on that date with Detective Inspector Brown, she just wanted to let it eat away at him for a couple of days, just like it had with Julia when they first met.

"I LOVE A HAPPY ENDING," SAID SUE WHEN THE CAFÉ finally closed just a little after midnight. "Promise me you won't get involved in another murder case?"

"I'll try not to."

"That's not the same as a promise."

"None of us know what's around the corner," Julia said. "Although Barker asked me out on a date."

"And you said yes?" Sue gasped, clutching her hand over her mouth. "I *knew* he liked you!"

Julia thought back to the almost kiss at the gallery earlier in the night, and she was surprised her gran hadn't already told Sue. Perhaps that was one piece of gossip she would keep to herself until Julia was ready.

"I didn't say yes," Julia said. "But I will."

"That's still a happy ending in my eyes," Sue said as she leaned in to kiss Julia on the cheek. "I'm going to go home and snuggle up to my husband and let him know he's the luckiest man in the world to have somebody like me, and not somebody like Rachel Carter as his wife. Goodnight, love."

"Goodnight," Julia said.

"Oh, and thank you for not telling the police I was the one who slashed the painting," Sue said as she walked through the beaded curtain. "I saw that awful flower and I was sure it was worthless."

She watched her sister walk through the messy café, and for the first time since Julia had opened the café, she was going to leave the clearing away for the morning because there was something else she needed to do for things to truly be a happy ending.

JULIA ALMOST FELL ASLEEP IN A CHAIR IN THE DARK corner of her stone yard behind her cafe, so when she saw the shadowy figure creeping through the night, she bolted upright and forced herself to wake up.

"Hello again, Jessie," Julia said.

Jessie sprung up from picking up the box of cakes Julia had left as bait. She glanced from the gate to Julia, but she didn't run. Julia opened the back door of her café and invited Jessie into the light.

After pulling down her hood and letting her dark hair fall forward, and eating an entire victoria sponge, Jessie sat back in her chair and looked around the café, a lot more at peace than she had seemed before.

"I have an offer to make you," Julia said. "It's a little different from the last one."

"I'm listening," Jessie said, staring down her nose the way she did.

Julia pulled out the chair across from Jessie and sat down. When she put her hands on the table and locked them together to stop them from shaking, she realised she was more nervous now than she had been hours earlier staring at Rachel's glittering blade.

"The room you stayed in at my cottage," Julia said, looking Jessie directly in the eyes. "It's of no use to me and I rarely have guests. How would you like to rent it?"

Jessie arched a brow and immediately started laughing. She shook her head and leaned across the table at Julia, her dark hair falling over her hazel eyes.

"Don't you remember, lady? I'm homeless. I don't have money."

"I know," Julia said, nodding carefully. "That's why I'm offering you a job here, in my café. I'll pay you a fair wage, and I won't charge much for the room, just enough for the upkeep. We'll have to contact social services, but I'm sure we can come to some sort of arrangement."

Jessie stared at Julia, and she wasn't sure if she was going to burst out laughing again, or make a run straight for the door; she did neither. Instead, she stared down her nose directly at Julia for the longest time.

"You mean – *like* – foster me?"

"If that's what it takes, and if it's okay with social services, then yes."

Julia had come up with this plan the night Jessie had slept in her guest bedroom, she just hadn't been sure she wanted to go through with it until tonight. Roxy's words had made her see that family is who you choose to be with, not who you are forced to. Jessie hadn't found a family, and Julia hadn't had the children she thought she would, but she could see the good in Jessie, even if Jessie couldn't.

"I'm not good," Jessie said. "I've done stuff."

"I know," Julia said, pulling out the piece of paper Barker had given her earlier that day. "All of this, it will need to end. That is my only condition. You treat me with respect, and you get it right back. What do you say?"

Jessie didn't say anything. She jumped out of her chair and wrapped her arms around Julia's neck. It took Julia a moment to realise what was happening, but when she did, she wrapped her arms around Jessie and hugged the girl she doubted had been hugged for a long time.

"Thanks, lady," Jessie whispered.

"Is that a deal?"

Jessie pulled away, tear streaks marking her dirty cheeks. She nodded furiously and held her hand out. Julia accepted it, and she was surprised by the strength of Jessie's grip.

Julia didn't know what the future held, but for the first time since arriving back in Peridale, she didn't feel like she had a weight looming over her. She knew that when she got home, the first thing she would do was face reality and open her divorce papers.

Julia pulled the '*HELP WANTED*' sign out of the window and looked down at it. She glanced over to Jessie, who was tucking into more cake. It was going to take a lot of hard work to get Jessie ready for working in the café, but if she enjoyed baking cakes as much as she enjoyed eating them, Julia knew they would be just fine.

"Come on, Jessie," Julia said as she opened the door. "Let's go home."

THANK YOU FOR READING
&
DON'T FORGET TO REVIEW!

Wow! I had a great time introducing you all to Peridale, and I hope you enjoyed reading it as much as I enjoyed writing it! If you did enjoy the book, **please consider writing a review.** I appreciate any feedback, no matter how long or short. It's a great way of letting other cozy mystery fans know what you thought about the book. Being an independent author means this is my livelihood, and *every review* really does make a **huge difference.** Reviews are the best way to support me so I can continue doing what I love, which is bringing you, the readers, more fun adventures in Peridale! *Thank you for spending time in Peridale, and I hope to see you again soon!*

The next book in the series, **Lemonade and Lies** is *OUT NOW!*